Girl in Luv

JAY CROWNOVER
and
REBECCA YARROS

Copyright Girl in Luv © 2019
by Jay Crownover & Rebecca Yarros

All rights reserved. No part of this publication may be reproduced, distributed or transmitted in any form or by any means, without prior written permission.

A letter of copyright has been applied for through the Library of Congress.

All rights reserved. Printed in the United States of America. No part of this book may be used or reproduced in any manner whatsoever without written permission, except in the case of brief quotations embodied in critical articles and reviews. For information, address Jay Crownover LLC, 1670 E. Cheyenne Mnt. Blvd. Box# 152, Colorado Springs, Colorado 80906.

Publisher's Note: This is a work of fiction. Names, characters, places, and incidents are a product of the authors' imaginations. Locales and public names are sometimes used for atmospheric purposes. Any resemblance to actual people, living or dead, or to businesses, companies, events, institutions, or locales is completely coincidental.

Cover design by: Mayhem Cover Creations
Editing and Formatting by: Elaine York, Allusion Publishing, www.allusiongraphics.com
Proofreading & Copy Editing by: Jenn Wood

Girl in Luv

They're from very different worlds...but their desire to be loved for who they really are is universal.

Langley Vaughn is in desperate need of a date.

But not just any date.

She's looking for a date to the wedding from hell. It isn't every day you're forced to be in the bridal party while your first love marries your archnemesis...otherwise known as the world's worst stepsister. The entire situation is a nightmare, and Langley is sick and tired of taking orders and forcing a fake smile. She's done being the bad guy when she was the one who was wronged.

She needs to find a date who's not afraid of her family's money...someone willing to shake things up. She needs someone outside of her normal social circle, someone ready to go to war with the well-to-do. She needs someone who won't back down. Someone willing to play the complicated game of tug-of-war she's been engaged in with her family for years.

Never in a million years did she think she was going to stumble across her very own heroic heartthrob when she set her crazy plan in motion.

Not only does Iker show up for her time and time again, he also forces her to finally fight for herself.

He says he's only there for the money...but his actions speak so much louder than his words.

Iker Alvarez would do anything and everything to get his hands on some quick cash.

Not just any cash, but enough to make sure his younger brother gets into the college of his dreams.

Thank goodness for a desperate, pretty little rich girl with too much money and her heart set on an outrageous scheme. Being in the right place at the right time might just be the answer to both of their prayers—and this smart soldier has never let a golden opportunity slide by.

Iker doesn't mind coming to Langley's rescue and being her plus-one...as long as the price is right.

Only, he didn't plan on liking the blonde socialite as much as he does. He is totally unprepared for the pull he feels toward her, coupled with his growing desire to protect her from the vultures and villains living under the same roof.

He wants to be the guy who keeps her safe and gives her the courage she obviously needs to fight back... But someone else, someone far more powerful and influential than Langley's wealthy family, has dibs on Iker's time and on his future. He knows he isn't the guy Langley can count on in the long run, but damn, if he doesn't want to do everything in his power to be that man.

Chapter 1

Langley

Red dress. Check.
Lip gloss. Check.
Respectable, sexy-but-not-quite-stripper heels. Check.

Cash? You betcha. I was pretty sure this wasn't the kind of bar where I would trust handing my credit card over to anyone to start a tab.

I was on a mission...as soon as I got out of this house.

"You're certain you can get them?" Virginia asked, clicking her manicured nails on the mahogany table. "Langley!" she hissed as I passed the archway that led to the dining room.

Damn. I'd almost made it out. For a split second, I debated ignoring my stepmother. Freedom was only twenty feet away. But I'd promised Dad I'd be the dutiful daughter this week, if only to make his life a little easier, so I looked longingly at the front door for another second, then turned into the dining room, clutching my keys so hard they dug into my palm.

"Don't leave yet. We need to talk to you," she ordered, then promptly went back to her phone call. "Right, I understand it's a last-minute change but we're paying you a lot of money to make sure she gets what she wants, and if it's pink peonies, then she's going to have pink peonies!"

What was that? The fourth flower change? The fifth?

I had no clue what they were paying the wedding planner, but it wasn't nearly enough.

"Move," Camille snapped from behind me.

I sidestepped and allowed my stepsister to pass, which was pretty much a metaphor for our entire relationship... or lack of one.

We'd both been freshmen in high school when our parents married. For that first year or so, I'd hoped we'd be friends, or even actual sisters. Instead, I ended up living across the hall from my biggest rival. Not just in grades, or sports, or college acceptances, but in *everything*.

But this upcoming wedding was the icing on her cupcake...or rather...her fancy French petit fours. Because a simple cupcake would never do for Virginia and Camille.

This weekend was what my stepsister saw as her ultimate win.

In just a few days, Camille was marrying my ex-boyfriend.

My stepsister took her seat at the twelve-foot table, which had been transformed into wedding central—or, as I like to call it, Ground Zero—and flipped through the seating chart binder.

Virginia hung up and rubbed her temples. "You'll have the peonies, Cammy."

"Thanks, Mom. I know they'll be beautiful." Camille hugged Virginia and a pang of longing stabbed me in the stomach.

I missed my mom. It had been nine years since cancer had stolen her from me—from us—but the longing and the sadness hadn't faded. If anything, watching how close Virginia and Camille were made Mom's absence echo that much louder in the big house.

"You needed me?" I prompted.

Two pairs of identical hazel eyes narrowed at me. It was eerie how much they looked alike.

"The wedding is in a week, Langley," Virginia said.

"Yes, I know." Of course I knew. I was pretty sure all of Colorado Springs and half of Denver knew.

"You still haven't given us the name of your plus-one." Camille pointed at the empty seat next to mine at the head table on the chart. "Is your new boyfriend's name that big of a secret? We haven't even met him."

Yep, that would be hard to keep a secret, since I currently didn't have one.

"Can you blame me for not bringing him around?" I asked her with a sweet smile while gritting my back teeth so hard they hurt.

Her very fake smile faded and two sets of disapproving eyes narrowed.

"Langley, honestly. I thought you were over this childish jealousy." Virginia sighed.

I bit back the first response that came to mind. It had four letters and rhymed with *buck*, which was, after all, exactly how I planned to secure said date for the Antichrist's wedding.

"Sorry, I'm just not sure if he can make it. I'm about to see him, so I'll ask." More like beg, plead, and bribe. But whatever it took, I was getting a damn date to this wedding.

"It's a week away, and he can't be sure he has the time?" Camille asked, her voice dripping with disdain.

"Well, not everyone's life revolves around your wedding." I shrugged. "I'll ask him tonight. And honestly, I don't see why I have to bring him." I knew Camille insisting I have a plus-one was simply to put me on the spot and make me feel even more awkward about the situation than I already did.

If I had a real boyfriend, I wouldn't exactly be jumping at the chance to introduce him to them. Chances were Camille might think I'd found someone better than Richard and try to change out her groom along with her flowers. After all, in her world, people and things were disposable and easily replaceable.

"Because if you don't, the table won't be even." Camille raised her eyebrows at me like I was the stupidest human ever. Which, I very well may have been. It took me far too long to realize she was scheming to seduce my boyfriend.

"Yeah, and we definitely wouldn't want that." I was usually better at keeping the sarcasm and resentment at bay, but the wedding madness had taken its toll lately.

Virginia tilted her head, and I waited for the scathing rebuff which usually followed any kind of outburst or action she deemed inappropriate and classless.

"Ladies, let's let Langley get to her plans."

A-freaking-men...Dad to the rescue.

"Of course. If you'll just let us know by tomorrow?" Virginia asked, her smile softening to the your-dad-is-here degree.

"Absolutely," I promised.

My heels clicked on the marble foyer as I quickly made my escape.

"Langley," Dad said softly, following.

I turned, my hand on the handle, his presence and approval the only things tethering me to this house at the moment.

"You okay?" He sounded worried. He always did when we spoke anymore. Or rather, when Virginia allowed us to speak.

Sighing under my breath, I muttered, "I told you I'd do everything I could to make this go well, and I will."

I couldn't meet his gaze as I told the blatant lie. I *didn't* want it to go well. And I'd been dreaming of a date to help with that plan ever since I was bullied into being part of the wedding party. I never lied to my dad...unless it had to do with his new family. I was an accomplished liar when it came to all things Virginia and Camille.

My father ran his hand over his salt-and-pepper hair and nodded. "I know you will. You always do the right thing. I hate that I had to ask you. I hate—" He dropped his voice. "I hate that you're being put through this."

Through what? Being forced to stand next to my stepsister in a pink bridesmaid dress as she marries the first guy I'd ever loved? Scratch that. First guy I *thought* I'd loved?

But that look in my father's tired eyes... For a second, I felt bad about my plan; not just about the lie, but the possible consequences of my deception.

"I know, Daddy." And I did. "I'm okay. By this time next week, it will all be over."

"Thank God." The man spoke the truth.

I grinned.

"Drive safe. And while I don't honestly care if the head table is symmetrical or not, I *am* excited to meet this boy. You've always been pretty quiet about your relationships, and no, I don't blame you, especially considering where we find ourselves at in this moment." At least he acknowledged this epic shit show. How could he blame me when the one boy I'd brought home ended up in Camille's bed only a few months later?

I let go of the handle and put both arms around my father. "I love you." I should say it more, but it was hard with Virginia and Camille always lurking around, ready to kill any kind of affection and tenderness between the two of us.

"Not nearly as much as I love you. Now get out of here before she makes you fold origami swans or something."

I kissed him on the cheek and fled.

Ten minutes later, I sat outside a little dive bar a few miles away from the gated walls of my neighborhood, nervously gripping my steering wheel. I'd driven past the place more than once on my way to my father's house. It always had a rowdy crowd gathered outside, and there were frequently police cars parked out front. It wasn't the kind of bar I would typically venture into, especially not when I was alone. But it was the perfect kind of place to find someone to mar Camille's perfect day. In fact, driving past this bar late one night was what gave me the idea to bring home someone she would absolutely hate having in all her precious wedding photos. I wanted to bring someone the other guests would be so interested in, they talked about him, and not how beautiful Camille looked in her expensive dress. At first, it had all been nothing more than a pipe-dream, but as the wedding grew closer, the more and more I envisioned how I could subtly exact my revenge for being lied to and cheated on.

"You can do this." I gave myself a last-minute pep talk, grabbed my purse, and headed for the bar. I'd never been to a place like this, and I was afraid it showed.

The bouncer looked me up and down as he examined my ID, then let me through the door. My heart pounded in time with the thought-stopping loud rock music coming from the live band on the corner stage.

The crowd was almost at capacity.

God, I wished I had brought one of my friends. Any of my friends, if I was being honest with myself. But it was June, so all of my college friends had already gone home for the summer, and I couldn't trust anyone who knew Camille, which excluded everyone I knew from high school. I couldn't change that reality, or the pathetic fact that Camille was marrying Richard. This was my world and I had to relinquish control over the things I couldn't change.

But I did have control over choosing who was sitting beside me during the reception.

I scanned the first table and quickly dismissed the guys sitting there when I saw the logo of a local golf course on two of their polos. They were exactly like the guys I went to high school with, exactly like whom I was supposed to show up with. They looked as out of place as I felt.

I didn't want safe and proper. Or rich. Or cotillion-educated.

I wanted someone who would make Camille and Virginia wish they'd never forced me into evening out their head table, or wearing that hideous pink dress, or expecting me to celebrate the marriage of my ex to my god-awful stepsister.

Maybe I'd have more luck in the back by the pool tables? I cringed when I glanced their way. Okay, there was a line between someone who looked like they might have gone to prison and someone who had actually *been* in prison. Those guys? Definitely of the second variety. I wanted to shake things up, not land myself dead in a ditch somewhere.

My legs were slightly unsteady as I crossed the room toward the long, wooden bar.

I took the only empty seat and ordered a drink, dismissing the bartender as a viable option as soon as I caught sight of his wedding band.

But out of the corner of my eye, I noticed the guy sitting next to me.

Holy shit, his arms were massive. And inked. Like, a lot. You didn't see that kind of tattoo work in the circles I normally ran in. I couldn't see his face since he was turned in the opposite direction, but his hair was close-cropped and very dark. Military, I guessed. We weren't far from Fort Carson, and there had to be at least a dozen GIs in here. Running into members of the military was rather common on this end of town.

The bartender slid my martini over, and I thanked him as I paid. Hopefully I'd have my choice made before

I needed another drink—or ten. I didn't want to have to Uber home and leave my car parked here overnight. I doubted it would still be there in the morning if I did.

Shifting my gaze to my other side, I found another possible option.

He was tall and lanky with shaggy, curly hair, tattoos up his neck, and more than a few metal pieces decorating his face. He was definitely cute in a very 'bad boy' kind of way.

Yep. He'd do just fine.

Actually, so would any of the other guys in his drinking trio. They'd give Virginia a coronary at first sight, not to mention, make for spectacular additions to the reception photos.

Okay, here went nothing.

"Hi," I said, because I figured something more cordial had to come out before *"Can I pay you to fake date me for the week?"*

The guy turned, his eyes sweeping over me and lingering on my breasts before meeting my eyes.

"Hello there," he answered with a smirk.

"I'm Langley," I offered.

"I'm Kyle," he answered...directly to my breasts.

Fake dating, I reminded myself. This guy sent my creep-o-meter up to level get-the-hell-out-before-he-wants-to-rub-the-lotion-on-your-skin. But, a girl had to do what she had to do when it came to getting revenge on her evil stepsister.

This was probably the moment when I should charm him with some dazzling small talk, but I didn't have the actual time for that, so I launched right into it.

"So, this might sound utterly insane, but I have a business proposition for you."

He snorted. "Oh, sugar, that's sweet, but I don't have to pay for sex."

My jaw hit the floor as embarrassment sent heat straight to my cheeks.

"No, that's not—" I shook my head. "You think I'm a hooker?"

He leaned back and assessed every inch of me, from toe to top. "That dress, this bar, and the smell of desperation? Yeah, it adds up to exactly that."

"What's wrong with my dress?" I looked down at the little, red sheath I'd picked up at Neiman Marcus. "You know what? Never mind. What the hell was I thinking?"

I slid off my barstool—which at five foot two was never a graceful motion, much less wearing this dress—while making my escape, and grabbed my purse off the bar. *To hell with this.*

Maybe I'd just have to beg one of my girlfriends to fly in for the weekend to balance out Camille's precious table, because this plan was obviously the dumbest idea in the history of dumb ideas. The jerk got one thing right, the desperation was making me act crazy and reckless.

"Where are you going?" Kyle called out as I made my way to the door.

I blew past the bouncer and headed around the corner into the parking lot, cursing my Louboutins with every step.

At this point, I was thinking that even Craigslist would have been a better option. What *was* I thinking, propositioning some guy at a bar like my life was a rom-com on Netflix?

"Hey, sugar, why the hurry?" Kyle's voice reached me at the same second his fingers wrapped around my arm.

Panic froze the breath in my lungs.

He spun me around, that smirk anything but reassuring. There was something *wrong* in his eyes, a hard glint that the darkened interior of the bar hadn't allowed me to see inside. He was easily a foot taller than I was, faster, too—especially with my heels—and the parking lot had shit lighting. He was no longer cute or a viable option.

He was a threat.

This was pretty much the opening scene of every woman's self-defense video I'd been shown my freshman year of college. I should have paid better attention.

"I thought you had a business offer for me?"

"Let me go." I tried to yank my arm free, but he only held on tighter.

"Come on, now. The night's just getting started. Why don't you take a ride with me, and we can talk about business?" The other two guys he'd been seated with silently appeared behind him.

"No!" I yelled as he pulled me closer.

"Come on, we know you'll like this kind of transaction," he promised.

I stomped down on his foot as hard as I could with my heel, and he shouted, but didn't let go. Stupid combat boots he was wearing. What was I—

A second later, a fist slammed into the jerk's smirking face, and I was free.

My heel snapped as I stumbled backward, landing hard on the pavement.

"She said no."

It was all my savior said, and all he apparently needed to say as he let his fists do the talking for him.

"What the fuck?" Kyle hissed from his position on the ground, touching his crooked, bloody nose. Oh yeah, that was definitely broken and well-deserved.

Good.

"She. Said. No," My rescuer repeated, taking a threatening step toward Kyle.

One of Kyle's friends charged, and my savior walked right into the advance, hitting him with another right hook. I gasped when the new guy took the skeevy friend by the throat and put him to the ground in one smooth move.

"You next?" he asked the third, his hand still gripping the second's neck. He wasn't even breathing hard, sweating, or anything. Calm as could be while my heart felt like it was going to jump out of my chest.

"Nope," the last guy said, backing away with his hands up.

My savior let go of the second asshole and stood up, putting himself between me and Kyle. "Like I was telling you, in case you didn't hear her or me each time you were told. She said no."

Kyle and his friend got to their feet while leaning on one another, and headed toward the third. Kyle's friend was definitely limping, and both of them were obviously bleeding.

"Fuck it, man. She's not worth it," Kyle muttered as the three disappeared back toward the entrance of the bar.

My rescuer turned toward me, and for a moment, I wondered if I'd just traded the frying pan for the fire. Holy shit, he'd just put two guys on the floor without breaking a sweat and now his gaze was fixed on me. I was still in the same parking lot with bad lighting... alone and unarmed. Why wasn't I scared out of my mind right now?

The dim parking lot lights didn't do much for revealing his face, but as he dropped down to face me where I still sat on the asphalt, I saw the arms—the muscles and the holy-shit-look-at-all-that-ink.

It was the dark-haired guy who'd been sitting next to me at the bar. The first one who had caught my eye but I'd not seen his face since he was turned away from me. The one I pegged as military from the jump.

"You okay?" he asked, all business. His voice was low with a little rasp to it. I really needed the shadows to shift so I could get a good look at him. If his face was half as nice as his voice, the guy had to be gorgeous.

"Yeah. Thank you. I just... Thank you." My voice shook, and so did my hands as I reached for my broken heel. I lifted my hand, studying the trembling fingers.

"It's the adrenaline. It'll wear off, don't worry. Let's get you some coffee. The shop right there is still open." He pointed to the opposite end of the parking lot.

"That's okay. I'm fine." There was zero warmth in his voice, and like hell was I going to escape one attack to only replace it with another.

"You're shaking, and it's not fine." He sighed. "Take out your cell phone."

"What?"

"Cell. Phone."

When I just stared at him, he took my purse, fished out my phone, and handed it to me.

"Open it."

Bossy!

I did, simply out of pure confusion, and maybe a little shock. At least I could call the cops if I had my phone in my hand. The thought was fleeting as he suddenly took it from me, snapped a selfie with the flash on, and then started tapping away with his thumbs. After a moment, he handed it back. Staring at the picture, I was stunned to see his face was even better than his voice. Gorgeous might not be good enough of a word to cover all the dark and dangerous swagger he was working with.

"My name is Iker. Iker Alvarez. I don't have a criminal record. I'm not going to hurt you, and you just told your"—he glanced down at the phone—"nine hundred and forty-two Instagram followers that we're going for coffee right over there." He pointed to the shop again.

"Why?" I asked, my voice still embarrassingly shaky. Iker? What kind of name was that? One I'd never heard before, but it suited his distinct, dark, good looks.

"Because you're as white as a ghost. My grandmother would kick my ass if she heard I left you sitting on the ground outside of a dingy bar after having almost been assaulted. Plus, with the way my life is going, I could use a hefty deposit in the karma bank." He handed my phone back to me. "You in?"

I nodded slowly, still kind of dazed and thoroughly confused at the turn this night had taken.

"Good." He glanced at my heels. "May I?"

I nodded again. Apparently, I'd gone from shaky words to zero words.

His grip was gentle on my foot as he removed my unbroken heel...and then *broke* it.

"And now you have flats. Let's go…"

I gawked at him, then my shoes. Who the hell was this guy?

He arched a dark eyebrow at me and lifted his chin a little. "This is the part in the story where you'll tell all of your friends you told me your name."

I blinked and stuttered, "Oh, Langley Vaughn." I couldn't believe the uneven tremble in my voice. I was never nervous enough I tripped over words or sounded shaky. I was an expert at hiding my emotions. Not in front of this stranger, apparently.

"Okay, Langley Vaughn, let's go."

I put on my butchered shoes and hobbled over to the coffee shop after him…because what else was I going to do?

Moments later, I sat across from him, sipping on a caramel latte.

He really was stunning. And not in a reasonably good-looking way. No, the man was may-I-climb-you-like-a-tree hot. He was maybe a year or two older than me with smooth, tanned skin, black hair cut in that telling high and tight style, dark eyes with thick, curling eyelashes, and lips I found more than a little distracting as he took a drink from the logo-embossed cup.

"You drink it black?" I asked, motioning to his coffee.

"Cream and sugar haven't always been available, so I got used to drinking it black." His eyes locked with mine as an awkward silence descended on us. "So, what was that all about? I saw you fly out of the bar like your ass was on fire after talking to that guy."

"Oh, I came to the immediate realization that I was pretty much an idiot," I admitted, proud that my voice had finally stopped trembling.

"How so?" There was no judgment in his eyes, just curiosity.

What the hell, right? I was more than embarrassed at my actions already. Who cared if he laughed me out of the coffee shop.

"I figured I could waltz into the bar, find someone who wouldn't mind fake-dating me for a week so I could make it through my stepsister's wedding, and it would all go off without a hitch." I laughed to myself before taking another sip of the latte.

"You need someone to fake-date you? Why?" He looked genuinely confused. "You can't find someone to go on a real date with?" He sounded skeptical.

"I can find a real date, but that's not what I need right now. My stepsister is marrying my ex-boyfriend in a wedding that's pretty much taken over my entire life, and I'm supposed to stand there in a fancy dress with a smile while she twists the knife a little deeper. Oh, and I need to identify my plus-one by tomorrow so I don't throw the head table off symmetrically." My lips lifted in a sarcastic smile as I air-quoted that last part. "I need the kind of date who doesn't mind ruining someone else's big day. Someone who can ruffle feathers and cause a bit of a spectacle, and this sounds awful when I actually vocalize it, but someone I would never date for real."

"Okay, that's all pretty fucked up." He laughed, and the sound warmed up the parts of me that were still numb from what had just almost happened in that parking lot.

It also revealed a lone dimple in his tanned cheek. Holy heartthrob Batman.

"It's not that funny," I argued. "Ridiculous, I do admit, but definitely not funny."

"Okay, so you wanted that tweaker to take you to your sister's wedding?"

"*Stepsister*," I corrected him. "And yeah. I wanted someone who would shock my family. Someone they wouldn't ever picture me with. Consider it my own personal form of revenge."

"I guess I just don't get it. You're a smokin' hot blonde with pretty blue eyes, who obviously favors the country club crowd, if the label on that purse and those trashed shoes are any indication. You should have dudes lined up around the block looking to help you out. Not be scouting out assholes in a grungy bar."

"It doesn't work that way in my world. Everyone I know also knows Camille, my stepsister, and Richard, my ex. Their wedding is a huge social event. No one would dare put a damper on their über-special big day. I need an outsider. A stranger." I didn't dare say this part out loud, but also someone unafraid of both my father's name and far-reaching influence and Virginia's well-known wrath.

"Got it." He nodded. "So, your plan was just to ask any random guy."

I nodded and blushed a little at the full truth. "I was planning to pay him. It's not like I was going to assume the pleasure of my company and whatever crab dish Camille finally agreed on serving would be enough to get someone to go along with my plan."

"How much?" he asked before taking another drink.

"How much what?" That dimple and those glinting dark eyes sure were *really* distracting.

"How much were you going to pay? I mean, how much does fake-dating run these days? Is it an hourly charge, a per diem charge, a flat fee?" He tapped his fingers on the side of his coffee mug and his eyebrows twitched as he watched me.

"Ten thousand dollars." I shrugged.

His hands spasmed in reaction, and for a second, I was sure I was about to be covered in coffee, but he held it in.

"I'm sorry?" he asked after he managed to swallow.

I played with the rim of my cup. "Ten thousand dollars," I repeated. "Seemed like a good, round number to convince someone to put up with my family's level of bullshit for the week."

"When does this week start?"

My eyes flew to his. "Monday, probably."

"When is this wedding that has taken over your life?"

I watched the play of tattooed skin over muscle in his strong forearms as he lowered his cup to the table.

"Next Saturday. But there's the rehearsal, and the family barbecue, and I figured I'd have to go shopping with the guy for a tux, so... Monday, I guess."

"And where is this wedding?"

"The Broadmoor." AKA, the golf club and resort I'd practically grown up at. The place I'd dreamed of getting married myself. I guess Camille won that one too.

"Holy shit. Your family's loaded."

"We're comfortable..." I repeated the phrase I'd heard countless times.

"Yeah, that's what loaded people always say."

"I guess that's true." Rich people only talked about how rich they were in the company of other obviously wealthy people. "It's my dad's money. Not mine. I'm a junior at Colorado College."

His eyes narrowed for a second, but not in an aggressive way. It was more of a thinking pose. "One more question," he finally said.

"Okay?" I wasn't aware we were having an interview.

"Did you love him? The ex?"

I swallowed, thinking of Richard. His wavy blond Ken-doll hair, his practiced smile. His black, traitorous heart.

"I thought I did, then. Now, I'm not sure if I honestly loved him, or if maybe my definition and scope of love wasn't what it should have been."

He held my gaze for several tense, electric seconds. I finally broke the connection, taking a sip of my latte. The way he looked at me made me shift in my seat. It was like he was searching for something, and knew he could find it if he just stared long enough. Like he could see past every layer to my very—

"Okay, I'll do it."

Now it was my turn to nearly spew caramel-flavored coffee everywhere.

It was a struggle, but I kept it down.

"I'm sorry?"

"I'll do it. I have most of the week off, ironically. Ten thousand dollars, a tux, and some decent food." He shrugged. "Why not?"

"Why would you? Not to use your own words against you, but you're smokin' hot and don't need to fake-date anyone." I said it with more bravado than I felt. Heat crept up my neck, no doubt leaving my face as crimson as my dress. I should be jumping for joy, not trying to talk this heroic super babe from helping me out.

He leaned forward, pinning me to my seat with those eyes.

"Because desperation takes all forms, Langley, not just pretty girls in red dresses slumming it at a shithole bar."

Well, that was slightly ominous, wasn't it? I blinked, thinking about it—thinking about having him for the week. Suddenly, this seemed more dangerous than picking up the creep in the bar.

"Or do I not seem like a bad enough guy for you?" he teased with the same grin he'd lit up my Instagram with.

My gaze drifted to his tattoos—the ones that started just above his wrists and ended somewhere behind his sleeves—and back to the single dimple that flashed on his cheek.

"Oh yeah, you'll do," I said softly. He'd more than do. He was perfect.

"Then, Langley Vaughn, you officially have a date to the wedding from hell, with the devil wearing a tux."

Chapter 2

Iker

Thank God for pretty girls with money to burn and no common sense.

I wasn't normally much of a drinker, but today I needed something to take the edge off. It was pure luck I wandered into the closest, cheapest bar to the base the same night this lost, debutante diva went in search of her revenge. I noticed her the minute she walked into the dark, dingy bar. She stuck out like a sore thumb, and it was easy to see her only reason for gracing the patrons with her presence was because she was going to cause trouble.

She looked nervous and unsure. Her eyes were wide and innocent, clearly looking for something she couldn't immediately identify. She was a rabbit who willingly walked into the center of a pack of hungry wolves, and it was only a matter of time before one of the predators lurking around tried to take a bite.

I was in no mood to play hero, or to be her entertainment while she slummed it for the night. She might be looking for trouble, but I'd spent the majority of my life trying to stay out of it. So, when the tiny blonde slid into the seat next to mine at the bar, I purposely turned my back on her. I felt her gaze like a physical touch when it skimmed over me and had to fight the urge to turn and see what color her eyes were, and if the shade of that siren's dress made them more vibrant. I was betting on blue. She had the whole girl-next-door thing going on. Well, as long as next door was located close to a members-only golf course and country club. The girl oozed money, which is why I'd inadvertently started paying attention when she said she had a business proposition for the tweaked-out metalhead sitting on her other side. I didn't want to be curious about anything having to do with her, but there was no getting around the fact anything having to do with money, and a quick way to get my hands on a lot of it, had taken up almost all of my available brainpower the last few months.

One of the scholarships my younger brother had been counting on to pay for college in the fall had fallen through, and now Gael was worried about being able to attend the school of his dreams.

My younger brother was twenty-times smarter than I ever was. The kid had endless potential and was destined to do great things with his life... as long as he had the opportunity and the bankroll. I was bound and determined to make sure he had every chance possible to succeed in life. I never wanted him backed into the same corners and harsh options I'd had to face for my own future. I supported both Gael and my grandmother who raised the both of us since I was fifteen years old. I couldn't remember a single day where I hadn't been hustling and

Girl in Love

busting my ass to take care of my family, but needing to come up with the cash to cover what the lost scholarship had taken care of wasn't something I'd managed to find a quick fix to. That is, until the tiny blonde walked into the bar.

Tapping my fingers on the side of my rapidly cooling coffee mug, I watched as Langley fidgeted nervously under my gaze. Even her name sounded expensive. We were from very different worlds. It was obvious at first glance. She came from money and influence. I was from a small border town way down in South Texas riddled with crime, violence, and a slew of bad choices. Never in a million years did we belong at the same table having a casual cup of coffee, but here we were. I needed to lock her down before she realized just how dangerous and careless her plan was to pick up a random stranger just to cause a little bit of chaos. I needed the money. That was my bottom line.

I pushed the coffee to the side and leaned forward, crossing my arms on the table in front of me. I watched her very blue eyes as they drifted to the tattoos decorating both of my forearms, and bit back a grin at the way she audibly gulped.

"Talk to me about the money." If I could get my hands on all ten grand by the end of the week, it would make everything else I had to deal with so much easier. Taking care of Gael was always priority number one, but I did have huge commitments to the army I was responsible for following through with on as well. I didn't take the uniform I wore lightly, or the duty that came with it. Like I said, there wasn't a day that went by where I wasn't hustling for one reason or another.

The young woman across from me cleared her throat and leaned back in the booth, making the vinyl creak and putting as much distance between us as she could. *Now* she was leery and hesitant. She certainly could have used some of those self-preservation instincts earlier. She shivered slightly in the slinky dress she was wearing, but eventually met my gaze.

"Meet me tomorrow at my family's tailor. I'll give you the first half if you show up, and the second half if you actually make it through the reception. I don't think you have any idea how elaborate and ostentatious a society wedding can be."

Hell no, I didn't. I didn't even know what the phrase "society wedding" meant, but there hadn't been many battles I'd lost in my life, so I doubted a fancy ass wedding was going to be one of them.

I shifted so I could pull my phone out of my back pocket. I unlocked the screen and pushed it across the table in her direction. "Put your number in. I'll text you so you have mine. Send me the info for the monkey suit shop and I'll be there."

I was a man of my word. Once I committed to something, I was all-in, especially when money was involved.

She tentatively picked up the phone and started tapping on the screen. I thought it was very cute the way her pale eyebrows dipped down in concentration. She was a stunning girl and there was a soft, delicate aura around her I found completely compelling. Nothing in my life had ever been easy, and softness of any kind wasn't something I typically ran across in my day-to-day. I was going to have to remind myself that Langley Vaughn was nothing more than a means to an end, if I didn't want to get even more tangled up with her than I already was, that is.

"You really have an entire week free to be at my beck and call? Don't you have a job or anything else you're responsible for?" She pushed my phone back across the table and tilted her head slightly to the side. "You don't look like the kind of guy who has a ton of idle time on his hands."

I grinned at her and watched as her eyes zeroed in on the dimple in my cheek.

"I'm in the army. So, yeah, Uncle Sam gets first dibs on my time, but this week I should be free, for the most part. Give me some specific times for the laundry list of events you listed off earlier and I'll do my best to make sure nothing comes up. For sure, though, I'll clear the day of the actual wedding and reception. We can negotiate the price if for some reason I can't make it to any of the other things you need me for."

She pointed to her own head full of long, gold-colored hair. "I wondered if you were a soldier."

The buzz cut was always a dead giveaway. Before I enlisted, I liked to wear my hair a little bit longer, but those days felt like a faded memory anymore.

"Yep. I enlisted the day I turned eighteen. I got transferred to Fort Carson a couple of years ago. I'm originally from a really small town in southern Texas." I rapped my fingers on the table and inclined my head toward her coffee mug. "You want a refill or you ready to go?"

I was going to walk her back to her car and see her off. There was no telling if the guy with the grabby hands and metal in his face was coming back with more reinforcements or not.

For a moment, just a split second, it looked like she hesitated. She couldn't possibly want to spend any more time in my company than was absolutely necessary... could she?

Naw. That was wishful thinking. This kind of girl wouldn't have anything to do with a guy like me if she had a choice. I knew it, and it wasn't smart to let myself think any other way.

"We can go." She looked out the window in the direction of the bar. "Would you mind walking back to my car with me?"

I nodded, not telling her that was already the plan. It was good to know she wasn't totally clueless when it came to being cautious. I didn't mind being the lesser of two evils of the male species in this particular scenario.

I flagged down the tired-looking waitress and paid for the coffee. Langley immediately protested, but I assured her that paying for coffee was well within my budget.

I shoved my hands in the front pockets of my jeans and slowed my steps to match her much-shorter stride. I hit right around six foot, so the top of her glossy blonde head barely reached my shoulder now that the heels were missing from her shoes. She clutched her purse so tightly her knuckles had no choice but to turn white, and her nervous gaze darted over to every shadow we passed through. She took a tiny step closer to my side, the events of the night obviously still not completely worn off, and I decided to distract her until we reached her car.

"What level of destruction are we talking about when it comes to ruining the stepsister's big day? Do you want me to object? Set the church on fire? Hit on the mother of the groom? How bad do you want things to get?" I couldn't afford to get myself arrested, but I could make a scene with very little effort if that was what she wanted. It actually sounded kind of fun. It'd been a long time since I was allowed to raise hell and get into trouble without fear of repercussion.

Langley let out a tiny snort and immediately lifted a hand to cover her face. "Uh... you really don't have to do anything other than show up. Believe me, that's enough to send Camille and her mother into a tizzy."

I paused a step and cocked my head to the side. "Because my last name is Alvarez?"

Was the fact I was Hispanic really enough to send her blue-blood family into a spiral? Hadn't we as a society progressed more than that after all these years? Some days it didn't feel like it, but I didn't need the reminder shoved down my throat. If I didn't need the money so badly, I would've walked away then and there.

Langley jolted to a stop and rapidly waved her hands back and forth. "No!" Her shriek was enough to wake up the entire city. I took a step back in surprise and felt my eyes widen as she advanced on me, unsteady in her broken shoes. "No. It has nothing to do with your last name. It's the tattoos and the fact that no one in our family's social circle knows who you are. People who come from old money are automatically prejudiced against anyone new. My stepmother will hate that a stranger is seated at the head table next to her precious daughter. It's as simple as that." She cleared her throat. "My father actually served in the army when he was younger. His father made all the boys in the family either enlist, or do volunteer work, in order to access their trust funds. All the girls had to enroll in college. He didn't believe anyone should have a free ride in life. He met my mother when he was stationed overseas. My dad will probably love you."

While I was trying to get a handle on what she was telling me, she gasped when she suddenly lost her balance and pitched forward. I caught her reflexively, seeing the truth in her eyes now that her face was so close to mine.

Sighing, I set her back on her feet and ran my hands over my short hair. "Okay."

What else was there to say?

I started walking again, keeping an eye on Langley to make sure she didn't fall again.

"You're as different from my ex as anyone can get, if that's any consolation." She cleared her throat and fiddled with her purse. "That's also a plus."

It was my turn to snort. "I would never get between sisters. Or stepsisters. You don't mess with family."

She made a soft sound. "I'm not sure that Camille gave him much of a choice. Anything I have, she wants, and usually gets. It was like that before her mom married my dad. For some reason, we've always been rivals. Getting Richard to propose to her was her ultimate win."

I shook my head and muttered, "It's only a win for her if you wanted to keep him, and it doesn't sound like you did."

She looked at me from under her long lashes and gave me a lopsided grin. "I'm not sure that I'm old enough or have lived enough life to know exactly what I want. For a while, though, I thought it was him." She shrugged.

"How old are you?" She had to be at least twenty-one to get into the bar and to be a junior in college, but she looked younger than that.

She gave me that uneven grin again and pushed her hair over her shoulder.

"I turned twenty-one at the beginning of the year."

She mentioned she was a junior at CC, which was a well-known private college, so the tuition was no joke. I'd learned all about how outrageous the cost of higher education was as soon as Gael started being placed in every advanced class the tiny high school in my hometown offered. I knew right away I had to do research on paying for college based on his curriculum in high school alone. Everything that came out of her perfectly painted mouth served as a constant reminder that we had zero in common.

"What are you in school for?" Did girls like her actually have to plan for the future, or did they simply get to waste money, knowing everything was always going to be taken care of in the long run?

"Economics."

What exactly did someone do with a degree in economics? Play with money? Invest in more stocks and bonds to get richer? Sock more money away for retirement? I seriously couldn't relate. Every dollar I made was already spent. Before I could ask for more details, she turned the tables and asked, "What about you? How long have you been in the army? You said you enlisted when you turned eighteen."

I nodded. "Yeah. I've been in six years. I went to Fort Knox for basic. Got stationed at Bragg, and deployed. Did a couple years at Polk, and ended up here. I'm a

Staff Sergeant now." Maybe for another year or so, then the Sergeant First Class list would be out, and I'd done everything to make sure my name would be on it. I maxed out my PT score at every test, stepped up when others backed out, and led my squad from the front, which had earned me more than a few ribbons for my dress blues.

I was good at taking orders, and even better at giving them, especially since I never asked my guys to do anything I wouldn't. My childhood had been anything but easy, so I was used to living in sparse and brutal conditions. I'd taken to being a soldier like a duck takes to water, and even though enlisting hadn't initially been what I wanted for myself, I didn't regret any of the choices I'd made to get where I am today. The military gave me a purpose and a solid means to an end regarding taking care of my family.

The conversation dwindled naturally as we reached the bar's parking lot and Langley's car. I waited while she dug her keys out of her purse, leaning on the side of the BMW. I watched as she pulled off the ruined high heels, wincing as her bare feet hit the asphalt. She turned to me and gave me a serious look.

"You're going to show tomorrow, right? This wasn't all some elaborate ploy, or joke that you're playing on me to make the out-of-place dumb blonde feel even more stupid?" She sounded so vulnerable, it did something to my insides.

I lifted my chin in agreement. "I'll be there, and I'll stick around as long you make good on your end of the deal."

She copied my chin lift, her blues bright enough to glitter mischievously, even in the darkened parking lot.

"Believe me, you are going to earn every cent of the ten grand. Camille is a nightmare and her mother is worse."

I pushed off the car and shrugged. "Bring it on."

If she had any idea of the poverty and oppressive sense of doom and disaster I grew up in, she wouldn't think her high-class family was any kind of legitimate threat or obstacle.

I tapped my knuckles on the roof of the car and told her to drive safe. I almost pulled my arm out of her sudden grasp when she stopped me and whispered a nearly silent, "Thank you for saving me from that other guy." The unexpected tingle shooting all the way through my body at her touch caught me totally off guard.

I wanted to tell her "Anytime," but it would be a lie. The truth was, our paths normally wouldn't cross and it was sheer coincidence they had tonight. I wasn't someone she could rely on beyond this week or past the zeros in her bank account balance.

I shook free and headed in the direction of where I'd parked my truck.

I'd solved one pressing problem. However, there was no shaking the sinking feeling I just created another one that would be almost as impossible to deal with.

Chapter 3

Langley

"How's it going in there?" I asked Iker as I sat on the buttery-soft leather sofa, flipping through the loaded-down itinerary Camille had just emailed out.

There was zero chance in hell I was going to sit through tea with the ladies on Wednesday. Especially not with Richard's mother on the invite list. I'd show up for the barbecue, the rehearsal, and the actual wedding, but that was it. My sense of duty and agreed-upon self-flagellation ended then and there.

"I'm hoping this is the last one you're making me try on," Iker answered from behind the curtained dressing room.

"Let me see." He'd looked incredible in the first two, but those hadn't met with Oliver's approval. The tailor was nothing short of a perfectionist, and I trusted his critical eye.

Iker pushed aside the curtain and walked toward me with his arms spread. "Well?" he asked, spinning slowly.

Unh. It was seriously unfair how good-looking he was. I managed to close my mouth, prayed I hadn't drooled, and nodded. "It's...nice," I squeaked out. How the hell had I gotten so lucky to find him?

He was hot enough to turn heads and soak panties. I'd seen the evidence myself as we'd walked through the Sunday afternoon crowds. He'd definitely turned mine, which was something I needed to keep under strict control. I never would have met Iker under normal circumstances, and would have bet all the money in my trust fund that I wasn't anywhere near his type.

"Get up there," Oliver ordered, motioning to the pedestal as he came around the partition, hiding us from the rest of the store.

"I think this is the one," I said as Oliver walked a circle around Iker, tilting his balding head this way and that.

"Langley Vaughn, I've been dressing your father for the last twenty years. I'll tell you if this is *the one* or not." He shot me a look that made me feel like I was five years old again, sitting in this exact seat.

Iker met my gaze in the mirror and lifted his eyebrows. I nearly snorted, his expression was so funny.

"How does it feel?" Oliver asked Iker.

"Exactly the same as the last two."

"Well, this is a much higher-quality material, so I would hope you'd feel the difference," Oliver muttered, checking the fit.

It sure as hell looked like it fit great to me. The fabric stretched over his muscled frame, accentuating his broad shoulders and tapered waist. What was it about a tux that made an already gorgeous guy even hotter?

"You might need a little more room in the inseam," Oliver remarked, tugging gently at Iker's thighs.

"I might need you to back your hand off my inseam," Iker suggested drily.

It was his turn to receive the trademark Oliver look.

"I think this is it," Oliver told me. "But, it is the most expensive of the three by about a thousand."

"We'll take it."

Iker turned on the podium to face me. "The other two were just fine. You don't have to get the most expensive one for one night." There was no hiding the exasperation in his tone.

I stood and walked around him on the podium, admiring not just the fit, but the man. I was at eye-level with all the most important parts of him. He must have been a fan of squats, because his ass was—

"Langley, seriously. Get one of the other ones. That's a shit ton of money to waste on a tux for a single night." His eyes followed me, but he stood still, letting me look my fill.

Oliver scoffed. "Let me know what you decide." He disappeared into the front of the store.

"When you're deployed, and a firefight erupts, and you've got bullets flying everywhere, what kind of armor do you wear?" I asked, pausing to look up at him.

"Kevlar." His dark eyes narrowed.

"And you wouldn't dream of going out there without it, right?"

"Fuck no. That will get you killed."

"What about a lesser-quality armor? Would you settle for something that looked okay, and could maybe stop shrapnel, but wouldn't stop bullets?" I tilted my head.

"Of course not, but this comparison isn't remotely on the same playing field."

"It is," I assured him. "You've never been where we're going. I've never been through what you have. So, if I suddenly showed up in the middle of a firefight in Afghanistan, I'd hope you'd give me the best armor for the job I was about to face, and that's what this is. Those other tuxes are nice, but this one..." I let my fingers rub the material at his wrist lightly, careful not to graze his skin. "This one is bulletproof."

He stepped off the podium, leaving one of the shiny cufflinks I'd started to nervously toy with between my fingers.

"If you want me to stand out, to draw attention in a way that's going to make it obvious that you're waving a giant 'fuck you' flag, then why put me in something that helps me blend in?"

He was too smart and too observant. Those were questions I didn't want to answer.

Because he was beautiful in it.

Because I wanted to watch him in it all night.

Because being on his arm would distract me from the fact that I was watching the first guy I'd ever loved marry the first girl who had ever hated me. Hell, who still hated me.

"Iker, you couldn't blend in if you tried. Trust me. You're too much—" I let go of his cufflinks and waved my hands in front of his torso. "Too much everything. Besides, you looking better than any of the other plus-ones is bigger than a 'fuck you' flag. It's like a 'fuck you' banner behind a plane. Or skywriting a gigantic middle finger on their wedding day."

His lips lifted, and his eyes narrowed in a quizzical way, like he was trying to figure me out.

"What?" I asked, fidgeting with my hands. His sudden scrutiny was more than a little unnerving.

"You're not like anyone I've ever met," he said quietly.

The guy had a great poker face, because I had absolutely zero clue if that was a good thing or an awful thing.

"Thank you," I responded instead.

He laughed, the dimple making its appearance. *Lick it.* I shook my head. The hell would I be doing anything of the sort. He was an employee for the week, and I was pretty sure that qualified as sexual harassment. Then again, the way I'd just checked out his ass and all the other parts of him definitely crossed the line.

"So, can we get out of here?" He sounded so hopeful.

"Sure, as soon as he finishes fitting you for your suit."

"My what?" he asked, eyebrows raising.

"Unless you have one you're fond of? It's for the rehearsal dinner. You can't wear the tux to both events."

His jaw clenched once. Twice. The dimple looked sexy, even when he was irritated.

"I seriously need a full suit for the rehearsal?" Those words were a mixture of question and quasi-accusation.

"Well, yeah. What other option is there?" I finished the question slowly and steadied myself for any answer he might give—clearly even expecting *toga* to be an option he'd throw out.

"Shirt and tie," he suggested.

"Oh, of course!" I opened up my phone so I could email the itinerary to him.

"Finally, something normal," he muttered.

"You'll need those for under the suit, naturally. You'd look a little odd without it. Not that you wouldn't have the chest to pull it off. I've seen your arms, and can pretty much assume that's the status quo all over." I waved my hand in front of his torso.

He sucked in a deep breath and focused his attention behind me as his hands clenched.

"Shall we start?" Oliver asked.

"Ten thousand?" Iker whispered so only I could hear.

"Yep," I answered, just as quiet. "Plus, all the clothes are on me. Now you'll never have to rent a tux again!"

"For all the black-tie events I go to." The sarcasm was thick enough to choke a horse.

"It never hurts to have a well-stocked closet," I argued.

"So, a suit," Oliver interrupted, bringing over samples. "We need to choose quickly if you want these altered in time."

"Then let's get to it! Oh, and he might need a few polos and some casual slacks, too," I added.

"For *what*?"

"The barbecue, of course."

Our gazes met and held, frustrated browns facing off against smiling blues.

"Ten thousand," I reminded him with a bright smile. I'd already given him the first five grand to ensure he actually followed me into the formalwear store.

He sighed, then answered my smile with a forced one of his own.

"Bring on the polo shirts." He was going to lose it when I mentioned the khakis and dress shoes as well. Oh well. All was fair in love and war, and this game we were playing had a little bit of both running throughout.

"Miss Vaughn, it's good to see you. Are you joining your father on the course today?" the doorman asked as Iker and I walked into the golf club the next day. I had to give him credit, I wasn't sure he was going to show after the fitting yesterday. He was clearly out of his element and playing along was taking a concentrated effort on his part. He didn't bother to hide the sneer on his face when the valet took the keys to my Beamer.

"Oh, no, thank you, Tim. We're just here for lunch." Lunch lessons, really, but Tim didn't need to know that.

"Excellent. I hope you enjoy yourselves," he finished with a polite smile toward us both as he left us standing in the foyer.

"Not likely," Iker muttered, taking in the sweeping staircase that led to the second floor twenty feet above us, the large fireplace, seating area, and the floor-to-ceiling drapes.

Meanwhile, I took *him* in.

He wore a pair of olive dress shorts and a black polo—both of which he'd picked out yesterday at Oliver's. The fabric stretched across his muscles, dipping into the curves and hollows of his back, but left his arms bare, where ink covered the rest of his skin to the wrist. I wanted a closer look at the designs because I was curious about the things important enough to him, so much so that he was going to wear them on his skin forever.

"*This* is a golf club?"

I bit back my instinctive response of *well, yeah*, and looked at the room again, trying to see it through his eyes.

The seating arrangement in front of the hearth wasn't necessarily comfy as much as it was polished and coordinated. The banister gleamed and the ceiling felt cathedral-high.

"I guess it is a little much," I admitted.

"A little?" He sounded incredulous and almost judgmental.

"It's just...the club. It's where I learned to swim, took tennis lessons in the summer, golf lessons for one very long, very painful, six-week session." I shrugged.

He looked down at me with that quiet, intense scrutiny I was beginning to get used to. It seemed to appear whenever the differences between our worlds were made painfully obvious, yet neither of us wanted to draw any more attention to the situation. It was weird, but the look often left me feeling lacking in some way.

"Where did you learn how to swim?" I asked, leading him down the hall.

"The Y."

"Oh, that's kind of the same."

He stared at me.

"Well, they both need memberships, right?" I muttered.

He didn't dignify that with a response as his hand spanned the small of my back, guiding me to the right of the walkway as a group of golfers passed.

More than a few heads turned, looking Iker up and down.

"Are you sure I don't need to get a long-sleeved shirt?" he asked.

"Nope," I assured him. "You're perfect just the way you are."

That damn dimple made another appearance at my comment.

We passed the pro shop, and then the expanse of glass doors that led out to the pillared terrace and putting green.

"I feel like I'm going to get kicked out," Iker mumbled.

"Over the tattoos? No way. Not with the exorbitant amount of dues my family pays to use the facilities. Besides, it's not like you're in jeans. *That* would most definitely get us kicked out," I promised with a nod as we came to the dining room hostess. "Hi there, Patricia, how is your day?"

Her smile was wide, and didn't falter when she saw Iker at my side.

"Miss Vaughn! My day is going well, and you?"

"Wonderful. We have reservations—"

"I've got you right here," she assured us. "If you'll follow me?"

She led us through the dining room, to a table that sat along the wall of glass windows. "Will this do?"

"Perfect," I assured her. We were still situated in a part of the dining room, but secluded enough for our purposes.

She nodded, and a waiter appeared, stepping forward to pull out my chair.

"Thank you," I told him as I sat, before he assisted with scooting in the wing-backed chair.

"I've got it," Iker told the waiter before he could approach his side, quickly seating himself.

"Of course, sir," the waiter remarked, quickly blinking away his surprise. "Can I get you started with drinks before your courses arrive?"

"Lemonade, please. Thank you...Michael," I finished after reading his engraved name tag.

"I'll have a Coke. Thank you," Iker ordered, tugging at his collar.

"He wasn't going to seat you," I told him, my lips quirking upward as Michael left.

"Yeah, I figured that out." He studied the golfers on the putting green for a moment before turning back to me. "Courses?"

"I had them change up the menu so you'd get the full experience of over-indulgence that you'll be confronted with this week."

"Are you trying to train me?" One raven eyebrow quirked up questioningly. "I'm not a pet. And last time I checked, I was already housebroken. You know that, right?"

"I'm sorry?" I adjusted the fabric of my sundress to keep my legs from sticking to the leather chair.

"You want to shock your family. We've already covered that." He leaned forward on his elbows, narrowing the distance between us.

"Okay?" I couldn't help but lean in too, keeping my hands folded in my lap.

"So, why train me? Why the lunch? The golf club? I checked the itinerary and this isn't on it." Again, he was too smart, quick to pick up on things that weren't explicitly laid out in front of him.

Because I'd wanted to see him again, for starters—not that I was going to say that. It was one thing to hire a fake date, and quite another to actually like him and want to spend time with him outside of the monetary obligations.

"I thought you might like a glimpse of what you're walking into." I gave him the partial truth. "And as for *training*, there's a big difference between making them uncomfortable"—I nodded toward the dining room—"and having *you* be uncomfortable."

He glanced at our dining companions, none of whom were interested in us. "Jeans will really get you kicked out?"

"Club rule." I shrugged.

"Ok, Country Club Girl. Teach." His dimple appeared as he grinned at me.

My chest stuttered, which reminded me to breathe. He was unlike anyone I'd ever been attracted to, and yet made me wonder how in the hell I'd ever found Ken-doll-types appealing. Iker was about a hundred times more fascinating, and I'd only known him a few days.

"Elbows off the table," I ordered.

He laughed, but did it, moving his forearms to the upholstered arms of the chair. "Too easy."

"Oh, yeah? We'll see how you feel in about an hour." I smirked.

"Challenge accepted."

It was on.

Dishes started arriving, and my back straightened, eight years of cotillion and etiquette courses kicking in.

"This one," I corrected him as he reached for his salad fork. I picked up the tiny-tined shrimp fork and waved it.

"That's too small," he argued.

I arched an eyebrow, and he picked up the shrimp fork, grumbling as he started in on the appetizer.

"Outside in," I instructed him with silverware. "Tear each individual piece of bread from the roll before buttering."

That one got me a set of rolled eyes.

By the second course, I thought he was going to quit.

"It's cold!" he sputtered, putting his spoon back in the soup.

"It's supposed to be," I told him.

"Tiny forks. Cold soup. What the hell is *wrong* with rich people?" he questioned, shaking his head. "My *abuela*'s menudo is way better than this."

"Elbows," I reminded him, and he promptly withdrew them. "Spoon the soup away from you, that way it won't splash your clothing." I demonstrated.

"Not a problem, because I'm not eating that shit—stuff," he corrected himself when an older gentleman glared at us.

I laughed, barely covering it with my napkin.

The meal passed with frustrated sighs—his—and laughter—mine. He caught on quickly, his eyes flickering back and forth over his place setting, taking in the details.

"How the hell do you remember all that?" he asked after we'd finished. "How can you even enjoy what you're eating with all those rules?"

I signed my name on the bill that would go directly to our membership account.

"Years of instruction. Practice. I wasn't allowed into a formal dining room, even out in public at formal functions, until I'd mastered it." I shrugged.

"Soup and everything?"

"Soup and everything," I confirmed, trying to recall. "I think I was nine before my parents permitted it." I'd been so proud, my back straight as I sat in that seat, feeling like an adult.

"You knew all of this by nine?" he questioned, rising from the table.

"For the most part."

Iker waved off the waiter and pulled out my chair himself.

"You learn incredibly fast." I stood, smoothing my hemline.

"I do," he agreed.

"And you're so humble," I teased as we crossed the dining room. Sure, there were stares—how could there not be? Iker was huge, tatted up, and walked like a predator, aware of everything and everyone around him. "Sorry about the stares. Maybe the tattoos are a little much for this crowd."

He looked down at me, the skin between his eyebrows puckering. In laughter or astonishment, I wasn't sure.

"I happen to like them," I admitted, heat creeping up my neck. It was the curse of being blonde and pale. It was hard to hide your emotions when your own body set itself off like a rising thermometer.

"You think it's just the tattoos?" His tone was arctic cold.

Now it was my forehead crinkling as we walked toward the foyer of the club.

"I stood out like a sore thumb. Hell, the only other guys who looked like me in that room were wearing name tags."

I blinked.

"It's okay," he said softly. "I knew what I was getting into. I'm going to hit the john. You okay here?"

I nodded. Of course I was okay here. This was where I fit in, almost like a second home.

A group of girls came out of the pro shop, all smiles and shopping bags. Their tennis skirts were all the same length. Their shirts may have been different colors, but they were all sleeveless polos. All five of them wore white Broadmoor sun visors with their high ponytails bobbing back and forth.

They were all variations of the same cookie, made with the same Stepford-shaped cutter.

"Oh my God! Langley!"

And apparently, I was also one of them, just dressed in different attire today.

The girl in the center raised her arms, bags included, and ran on her tiptoes over to me.

"Nessa," I said in greeting as she kissed my cheek.

"Where have you *been*?" she asked, her perfectly aligned teeth whiter than snow.

"Around? I go to CC—"

"We've missed you for doubles!" She ran me right over, and the other Stepfords nodded in agreement, like she'd pulled a string as their puppet master.

"Oh, I haven't been playing much."

Her face fell. "Oh, I understand. I wouldn't want to hang around here, either, if I were you."

My spine stiffened.

"I mean, how awful is it for you that Richard is marrying Camille? Is it super awkward at home?"

They all shifted, leaning in. Gossip was as valuable as gold with this crew.

"It's...fine," I responded, knowing if I said anything else, it would get back to Camille before the valet could pull my car around.

Nessa's eyes narrowed, deciding whether or not to believe me.

"Really. It's fine," I gave her my practiced, fake smile. "I'm in the wedding and everything. They're a perfectly matched couple and I couldn't wish anything for them other than my best."

At least that was the truth. They were both assholes who deserved each other, and my best was a giant "fuck you" in the form of a very tatted-up, military hottie who was coming out of the bathroom at any moment.

"But still, doesn't it grate on you a little? I mean, she's your sister!" Nessa dropped her voice to a stage whisper.

"Stepsister," I corrected her out of habit.

"And Richard was *the* catch of our class. He's going to law school and everything, right?"

Damn, the girl was digging deep for the dirt, but I wasn't going to give her even one granule of sand.

"He's still a junior in college, just like the rest of us." How could someone who was only twenty-one be defined as *the* catch?

"Right, right, but all of us just thought that it would be you two until the end of time!"

If I got any stiffer, I was going to snap like a brittle twig. What was it about bitches who needed to pick at scabs? Were they hoping that seeing my blood would make their own wounds and insecurities hurt a little less?

"Well, thank God they didn't last, otherwise I would have missed out," Iker's voice came from behind me just a second before his arms pulled me back against his very firm chest, wrapping just under my breasts, his tats on full display for their wandering eyes.

My entire body melted because I was suddenly boneless from his touch.

Nessa's eyes widened, and the others followed suit. Their gazes lingered on his tattooed arms, the muscles rippling as he adjusted his hold on me.

"Oh my," Nessa said softly. "Aren't you just..." Her gaze shifted to me. "No wonder you've been hard to peg down this summer. Rebellion looks good on you, Langley. And he most certainly looks better in person than he did on your Instagram."

I bristled.

"You ready to get out of here, baby?" he asked, ignoring Nessa and leaning down so his lips brushed my temple.

"Absolutely." My chest tightened. He smelled so good, like soap and a cologne I couldn't identify.

"I guess we'll see you girls at the wedding," Iker told them as he took my hand into his much larger one.

I said a quick goodbye as we headed out to the valet.

"What's wrong?" he asked while the valet ran for the car.

"They took one look at you, and thought they knew you." I shook my head. But hadn't I also done the same the first time I laid eyes on him? How he'd put himself in harm's way for a stranger in a dark parking lot. How he'd stepped up to help a stranger out. They thought he was nothing more than my rebellion...but wasn't that why I'd hired him? Wasn't that reaction exactly what I'd gone looking for when I found Iker? "They're all the same. All of them. Like assembly-line Barbie dolls, impossible to tell apart. And..." I shook my head.

He didn't push, just watched me with perceptive eyes, waiting for me to speak and admit the awful, self-reflecting truth.

"And I'm one of them."

"No, you're not," he said quietly.

"What makes you say that?"

"You came looking for me."

I scoffed. "Just to piss them all off."

He shrugged. "So what? You still came looking. You didn't jump Dick's best friend, right?"

"What?" My neck was at an almost impossible angle to look at him.

"Dick. Richard. Seemed fitting. You didn't fuck his best friend, did you?"

My lips parted. I couldn't think of one instance in the last twenty-one years when I'd heard that obscene word spoken in these hallowed halls, but I was all for hearing it again. Or using it as a verb. Or putting it into action. Whatever.

"No, of course not."

He nodded, then grabbed a few bills from his wallet as the valet handed him the keys to my car. "Thanks, man."

"No problem. See you soon, Miss Vaughn." The valet held open my door and I slid into the soft leather of my passenger seat.

Iker buckled in and put the car in gear, but didn't drive.

"Iker?" I asked, wondering what the hold-up was and slightly desperate to escape this place that so clearly highlighted our vast array of differences.

"Those women are all identical in a way," he agreed. "All a blur because they don't care to stand out. There's comfort in conformity—I get that." He swallowed, then turned to face me. "But you're not one of them. Maybe in some ways you are, sure. You're all highlighted with the same shade of money-green. But I can see you through the glow, Langley."

Emotion squeezed my throat.

"Me or my ten thousand?" I asked, trying to lighten the mood.

"You," he assured me.

I expected my hair to start flying from the static he caused, that's how electric the air felt around him.

"But that ten thousand isn't too bad either." He winked, and peeled out, leaving tire marks and open mouths in front of the golf club.

Chapter 4

Iker

"Are you sure you're going to be able to come up with the rest of the money by the end of the week?" Gael's voice cracked through the speaker of my cell and I could tell he didn't want to get his hopes up too high. Disappointment was something we were both well acquainted with, which meant I would sell my soul in order to come through for him. No matter what it took.

"I told you not to worry about it. When have I ever not come through when I promised you something?" I tried to keep my voice light, but my heart dropped into my stomach when I pulled up in front of the sprawling, extravagant home tucked away in the old, rich neighborhood of the Broadmoor. I knew Langley's zip code came with a big ass house, but I'd underestimated just how big. "I'll have the rest in no time."

Gael sighed and I could picture him shaking his head. We looked a lot alike, though he was much softer and gentler all around than I was. I liked to think I was the buffer between my brother and the harsh realities of our childhood, which allowed him to grow up without all the sharp edges and pointy, protective pieces I'd developed along the way.

"You didn't do anything that's going to get you in trouble in order to pay for my school, did you?" He sounded nervous again because he knew me well. There wasn't much I wouldn't risk to provide for him and my grandmother.

I swallowed as I found an empty spot in the huge, circular, brick-lined driveway in front of the old, Victorian mansion. My pickup towered over the low-slung sports cars and luxury sedans filling up the rest of the available space.

"Depends on your definition of *trouble*." My unwanted attraction to Langley Vaughn was proving to be much harder to ignore than I anticipated. "It's actually kind of a funny story. I'll tell you next time I see you."

"When will that be?" Now Gael sounded sullen and bratty. Admittedly, I hadn't been home as much as I would like, but my job was unpredictable at the best of times.

"I'll come and see you when I get..." My sentence was cut off when the giant, wooden front doors of the house swung open and Langley came running out. It seemed like she'd been waiting for my arrival. I let out a little grunt of surprise when she suddenly ran toward me, throwing herself into my arms and nearly strangling me with a hug around my neck as soon as she was close enough to touch.

"Hey." My greeting was less enthusiastic than hers. I put a hand on the small of her back when I felt the way her lithe frame was shaking against me.

"I really wasn't sure you were going to show. I thought the cold soup might have been the last straw." She was trying to make a joke, but when I pushed her back a step, I could see how tense she looked.

I pointed at my phone and the call still connected to my brother. "Give me a sec." She nodded and I turned my attention back to Gael. "I gotta go. Tell Gram not to worry. Everything is under control and I'll be home soon." But not soon enough. It never was.

Gael snorted. "I miss you. Stay out of trouble."

I muttered a goodbye and tucked my phone in my back pocket. I turned my attention back to Langley, only to find her pacing in front of me, tugging on her bottom lip. She was always kind of high-strung, but today she seemed especially fragile. It looked like one wrong move would make her break.

"You okay?" She was really good at hiding what she was feeling behind a very practiced smile, but today, there wasn't even a fake smile to be found.

She stopped her aimless marching and let her hands drop to her sides. I watched as she visibly pulled herself together.

"I'm okay. I've been fielding a million questions from literally everyone about you all day, ever since I announced that you were coming. It was a little stressful. Plus, Richard's entire family is here. Do you know how awkward it is to have both the mother and father of the groom offering their condolences every time they walk past?" She shook her head. "Not to mention, Richard's mother has told me no less than four times that 'Camille is simply a better match.' I swear, I'm at my breaking point."

I grunted out a sympathetic sound and let her wrap her fingers around the inside of my elbow. I'd worn one of the damn polo shirts she insisted on, but you would have to bury me before I put on a pair of khakis. I was wearing black jeans, the only pair I owned which didn't have a hole in them. Hopefully they let me through the front door.

"Sounds rough. Point her out to me and I'll be sure to mention she looks like someone I know back home... only much older."

Langley giggled and looked up at me from under her lashes as we made our way to the front doors. The old house was massive and I felt like I was stepping back in time.

"I'll point her out, and everyone else you might want to avoid. They all want to know about your family and background. It's best to steer clear if you don't want to end up answering leading questions." She sounded apologetic.

I shrugged. "Let them ask. I don't have anything to hide." And I'd long gotten past being ashamed of where I came from. "There isn't much to tell. My family is small. Just me and my brother. Our mother bounced in and out of our lives until Gael was five, so it was primarily our grandmother who raised us. Neither one of us ever met either of our fathers. Gael still lives with my *abuela* in Texas. At least he does until he leaves for college. That was him on the phone. He was making sure I could cover his first semester's tuition for him."

She paused a step and her expression changed from worried to thoughtful. "You're paying for your brother to go to college?"

I nodded and reached for the door. "Yep. He's hella smart. He's one of those kids who's going to change the world if he has the proper tools. I promised him he could go to whatever school he wanted. Financial aid covered a solid chunk, but the rest is all on me." And it would be until he graduated.

She didn't ask if the ten grand was going toward my brother's education, but she was a bright girl, so I bet she was able to put two and two together pretty fast. Her fingers tightened on my arm and her voice was slightly breathy as she whispered, "You're kind of amazing, did you know that?"

I gave her a grin. "Depends on the day." I had some pretty good qualities, most of which my grandmother had drilled into me. I had some pretty bad ones too, but I did my best to keep them reined in.

She nudged me with her elbow and pulled me to a stop before we entered the opulent foyer. "My dad asked where we met. I told him I had car trouble and you stopped to help out. I didn't go into much detail, but everyone knows we've only known each other for a short time. I told them you were in the military, which is why it was hard for you to commit to being my date before now." She shifted slightly on her high-heeled sandals. "I also made it clear we are casually dating. I figured I would save myself the headache of trying to explain why you're no longer around once the wedding is over. Don't let my dad corner you and ask what your intentions are toward me. He can be a little overprotective."

I put a hand over her increasingly tight hold on my arm. There was a slight tremor making her fingers shake, and I was momentarily blindsided by the desire to protect her. I didn't have time to be her hero, but damn, if I didn't want to try.

"Everything will be fine. We'll go in, schmooze, piss your stepsister off, and call it a day. Don't worry about me. I got this." At least I could pretend to have this. No lie, though, the house was insanely intimidating, but I didn't give a shit about anyone inside of it. The girl next to me was my priority—and my job—and that was what I was going to focus on.

I heard Langley suck in a breath and again watched as she visibly prepared herself for battle. The plastic smile was locked in place and her pretty blue eyes went flinty and cold. She became an entirely different person in that moment. I preferred the quirky, self-deprecating girl I'd spent the last few days with, not this alter-ego version. This icy socialite was not someone I would ever choose to spend my limited free time with if given the opportunity.

Langley faltered a step as an older woman suddenly appeared from around a corner.

"I thought maybe you got lost, or had to go find a date on the street, you were gone so long. Come to the garden. Everyone is waiting on you to start eating." The woman barking the clipped orders was lurking just beyond the entryway, as if she'd been waiting for Langley to come inside just so she could pounce on her.

I lifted my eyebrows at the Real-Housewife-of-Colorado Springs, and watched as she barely concealed a shiver of distaste when she finally caught sight of me. The woman was wearing the kind of jewelry I'd only ever seen on celebrities going to the Oscars, and dressed like Lucille

Bluth from *Arrested Development,* even though she was a decade younger. Can you say, 'trying too hard'?

Langley sighed and shifted a little closer to my side. "Virginia, this is Iker Alvarez. He's going to be accompanying me to the wedding."

I felt the woman's calculating gaze drift over the tattoos on my arms, and watched her sneer when she caught sight of my jeans. When she met my gaze, there was nothing but contempt and scorn in her eyes. I felt a chill dance down my spine, and instantly understood why Langley had been so crazy desperate for someone to shield her from this woman's wrath.

"You explained the wedding has a dress code, I assume?" Her disdain switched to Langley and I felt her flinch.

"How about you say 'hello' instead of worrying about the dress code?" The response was spoken softly, but the older woman recoiled like she'd been shot. Apparently, Langley wasn't one who usually snapped back when attacked. It was almost worth the silent scorn to see the look of shock that crossed the bitchy stepmother's face.

The older woman sniffed and turned on her heel. "Don't waste any more time. Today is about Cammy and Richard. Stop trying to make it about you."

I watched with wide eyes as the woman stormed away, heels clicking on the hardwood floors in an angry rhythm.

"Wow." The word escaped before I could stop it. Langley gave me a panicked look, so I shrugged. "She's something else, isn't she?"

"I wish I could say it'll get better, but it won't. Camille is exactly like her."

I'd been in war zones more welcoming.

I nodded and let Langley guide me down the hall. I was trying not to gawk at the artwork, which I assumed were originals, lining the walls and the obviously expensive and antique furniture filling the rooms we walked by.

"If she's that bad, what did your dad ever see in her? If he's overprotective, how can he stomach the way she speaks to you?" It didn't make any sense.

Langley sighed. "When my mother passed away, my dad was devastated. They had a once-in-a-lifetime kind of love. He really lost himself, and his interest in almost everything and everyone around him. Including me."

She shook her head a little, the ends of her long blonde hair brushing across my bare arm. It felt like silk and I wanted to grab handfuls of it and bury my face in it. Oh yeah, there was definitely more than one kind of trouble to get into when this woman was involved.

"Virginia moved in on him when he was still grieving. I think she saw he was vulnerable and took advantage of the situation. But, she made him happy. She pulled him out of his funk and forced him to start living his life again. She and I never clicked, and you already know how Camille felt about me. None of that mattered, though, because my dad was happy. Generally speaking, we keep the animosity to a minimum. During the school year, I don't live in the house, so that helps some."

I wondered if she called this monolith of a house home, because it felt anything but homey to me.

"Where do you stay during the school year?"

She lifted an eyebrow and finally flashed a real smile. "Guess."

I snorted out a little laugh. "In a sorority house." It wasn't that hard to figure out.

She tossed her head back and laughed. "Yep. Got it on the first try."

Of course she was in a sorority. It was just one more thing separating her from everything I'd ever known. The only time I'd stepped foot on a college campus was when I'd gone to tour a couple local campuses with Gael.

Langley tugged on my arm, trying to quicken the pace. I gently pulled free and waited until she stopped and turned to face me. I rubbed a hand over my chin and cocked an eyebrow. "She wants us to hurry, so we should make her wait. I'm sure she's already out there telling everyone about the heathen you brought to sully their pristine garden party. Let her stew for a little bit. It'll be fun."

Langley looked uncertain. It was obvious she was used to keeping the peace inside these walls. But, she hired me for a reason, so even if she didn't want to rock the boat, I was here to do more than just make some waves...I was ready to sink that ship. Deciding to give her a built-in excuse for not following orders like a docile little lamb, I asked her to show me where the bathroom was. There had to be several on this floor alone, and God forbid I use the wrong one or wander into a room that was just there for looking at. I was pretty sure all rich people had one of those.

With obvious reluctance, she pointed me down another hallway and told me she'd wait for me. I could tell she was anxious about directly defying her stepmother, but after hearing how the woman treated her, I knew it was long past time for this Cinderella to shake things up, so I made my way as slowly as I possibly could toward the "facilities," as I'm sure it would be referred to in proper social circles.

"Richard...everyone else is right outside. You need to stop." The female voice brought me to a halt mid-step and I felt my eyes widen. It could be a coincidence that the soon-to-be-groom shared the name Richard with the dude pressing up on a pretty, dark-haired girl I thought I recognized from the golf club yesterday. "Camille will kill us both if she catches us."

Not a coincidence. The blond guy in the polo and khakis was definitely the groom. Well, wasn't that something? It looked like Langley wasn't the only Vaughn he was stepping out on. This whole situation really was like something out of an outrageous reality TV show. This guy was bold. His entire family was a few hundred yards away, waiting to celebrate his upcoming wedding, and he hadn't even bothered to close the door to the bathroom before throwing his moves on the chick he had pressed up against the vanity.

I cleared my throat and motioned to the bathroom behind them.

The blond guy stepped away from the brunette. The girl audibly gulped and gave me a little finger wave as she practically bolted down the hall. She tossed a hurried, "Nice to see you again," over her shoulder, and I watched as she practically plowed into Langley, who was hovering at the end of the hall.

The sleazeball smoothed a manicured hand down the front of his pressed polo and gave me a narrow-eyed look. The watch on his wrist cost more than my truck, and I felt a nearly uncontrollable urge to put my fist in his perfectly straight and polished smile.

"Who are you? What are you doing in the main house? Don't you know the help has a separate entrance?"

The help?

Oh yeah, someone needed to beat his ass. And enlighten him. The people calling the shots in the world now all came in a variety of shapes, sizes, colors, and genders. His antiquated thinking was laughable and needed an adjustment. It was a shame I wasn't going to be the one to tweak his worldview.

"I'm Langley's date." I smirked at him and crossed my arms over my chest. I didn't look the same way he did in a polo. Thank God. "She obviously upgraded."

A sneer very much like the one I'd received from the stepmother crossed his face. "Seriously? What is that girl thinking?"

I rolled my eyes. "Probably that she wants to be with someone who isn't trying to stick his dick in everything that moves. Congrats on your wedding, by the way." My smile was more a baring of teeth. I couldn't believe someone as sweet and obviously as smart as Langley had fallen for this loser.

The preppy jerk sidestepped me and gave me a wide berth as he stomped off down the hall. Damn. I hadn't even been here for twenty minutes and I was already earning the cash Langley was forking over. It was much easier than I anticipated to make the upper crust angry.

I flashed Langley a thumbs up when she called my name from the end of the hall. I dipped into the bathroom for real, wondering if the candlesticks near the sink were pure gold or not. This was hands down the fanciest place I had ever taken a piss. Shaking my head at my own thoughts, I washed my hands with the smelly frou-frou soap and dried them on the monogrammed hand towel.

When I walked out of the bathroom, I was surprised to find a blonde leaning against the opposite wall, a blonde who wasn't Langley. No, this blonde was all long legs and predatory green eyes. She looked enough like the stepmother that it was easy to assume she was the infamous Camille.

Immediately on the defense, my spine stiffened and I narrowed my eyes in a warning look. I wasn't letting this chick close enough to touch. It was obvious she and the Dick were a match made in heaven if the way she was practically stripping me down with her eyes was any indication.

"Where is Langley?"

The stepsister pushed off the wall and gave me a smile that made my blood run cold.

"Taking care of something for me. She can't tell the bride 'no' this close to the wedding. I saw your picture on her Instagram. I didn't believe you were actually dating her. I had to come see what all the fuss was about for myself. You have all my friends thinking twice about using the fraternity on campus to find future husbands, and instead have them considering hanging out at the closest army base instead." She took another step toward me, but I was quick to dodge out of her way.

Man, maybe growing up in this house was just as dangerous as growing up in a border town. The weapons were different, less sharp and pointy, but the intent was the same. Take out the weak by any means necessary. Only, I didn't think Langley was weak. I thought she was kind. Her heart was far too soft to be in the care of these vicious women.

"Well, now you came and you saw. I'm going to go find Langley." Like, right now. I didn't want to spend any more time alone with this girl. "By the way, you should probably worry more about what your future husband is getting up to, instead of worrying about your stepsister's date."

A smile that was sharp as a switchblade crossed the blonde woman's face. "Oh, I know exactly what Richard is up to. How do you think I managed to lure him away from Langley?"

Vicious wasn't a strong enough word. This chick was lethal.

"I guess you two deserve each other then." I started to walk away when I felt the brush of her hand down the length of my spine. It made me shiver, but not in the good way.

I looked at her over my shoulder and cringed when I felt her fingernails drag across the nape of my neck.

"I deserve the best, but for some reason, Langley always seems to find it before I do. It's always so much fun—and so awfully easy—to take the best away from her."

Oh, hell no. I was here to play a game, but not this kind. Like I told Langley the first night we met... you didn't mess with family.

I really was going to have to do my best to protect Langley from these predators. But who was going to keep her safe once I was no longer around?

Chapter 5

Langley

"I can't thank you enough for your flexibility, Mandy." I finished the phone call with the spa, and then moved the Velcro-backed appointment card to an hour later on the movie poster-sized schedule for Friday.

Now, Camille wouldn't have to wake up at the "god-awful" hour of eight a.m. for the bridal party's morning of pampering. Who knew what had driven her to demand that immediate change, but hopefully Iker hadn't gotten lost while I'd been jumping through hoops for her.

The impulse struck to move every single appointment between now and the wedding, just to piss off Camille, but it would send her into a meltdown, which would send Virginia into a nuclear one, which would then rain down all sorts of hell on Dad.

Not worth it.

I walked out of the dining room rubbing my temples. *Just a few more days*, I reminded myself. Then all this wedding bullshit would be over, and with Camille and Richard on their honeymoon, I could finally enjoy the rest of the summer.

My stomach dropped at the thought of never seeing Iker again, though.

It was stupid, and I was more than aware of it, but I *liked* him. How could I not like a guy who was willing to put himself through torture to help his little brother pay for college? Ten thousand was a drop in the trust-fund bucket for me, yet it was life-altering for Iker's family.

I wasn't blind to the privilege of growing up with money, but it was hard to truly measure the real-world effects of something I'd always known...until I spent time with someone who'd had to work for every single thing he had.

My thoughts clicked along at the same rate as my heels across the polished floors. Maybe I could find out where Iker's brother was going. Maybe my trust fund could help out with a little anonymous scholarship. If he was half as smart as Iker said he was, and half as good-hearted as Iker was, it was a more-than-sound investment in the future of...well, humanity, I supposed.

It shouldn't be so hard for them when I had it so easy.

And besides, it would relieve a ton of stress off Iker's shoulders.

It also meant he wouldn't have to do something as desperate as find another socialite to fake-date.

Not that he would. Pretty sure he'd run screaming from my little zip code and the people in it the moment this weekend was over. Hell, even I wanted to.

"I deserve the best, but for some reason, Langley always seems to find it before I do. It's always so much fun—and so awfully easy—to take the best away from her."

I stopped dead in my tracks just outside the hallway that led to the powder room as Camille's grating voice reached me.

Knowing she took glee in hurting me wasn't a new revelation, but hearing her say it out loud was still a shock. I'd given her the benefit of the doubt when we were younger, knowing that she had massive daddy issues, and—quite frankly—wanted mine. It had made sense. Who wouldn't want my dad to be theirs? He was smart, and funny, and kind, and had a heart bigger than the state of Colorado.

But she hadn't been willing to share her mom, which was a sentiment Virginia wholeheartedly agreed with.

So, I understood it, her competitive nature. Her completely selfish drive to take everything I had. My mom had died. Her dad hadn't wanted her.

The two were vastly different.

But if she was talking to whom I thought—

"See, I'm not something that can be taken away from Langley."

Iker.

Oh, *hell no.*

She'd wormed her way into every facet of my life. Even dyed her hair the same shade as mine. And I'd let it slide.

But she couldn't have Iker.

A bolt of possessiveness hit my bloodstream like lightning, and my feet propelled me into the hallway before I'd even decided what to do.

"There you are, baby," I said to Iker as I strode down the hallway.

I pretended not to see the white ankle-strap Louboutins directly behind him, and the rest of her didn't require my imagination. Iker's massive frame simply blocked her out.

"Langley," he uttered my name with a sigh of relief.

I didn't stop until my hands rested on his chest, and before I could talk myself out of it, I rose on my toes to press my lips to his.

For being such a hard guy everywhere else, his lips were incredibly soft and full.

Iker didn't miss a beat. His arms came around my back to hold me against his chest as he kissed me back. It was light and simple, but his lips lingered over mine, gently sucking on my lower lip before he released me.

Okay, maybe it had been too long since I'd kissed a man, but honest-to-God tingles shot down my torso. My head spun a little and I couldn't stop my tongue from darting out to lick across my swollen bottom lip. As far as first kisses went, this one was gonna rank at the top of my best kiss list for a very long time, and it hadn't even been real.

"Langley, did you get those reservations changed?" Camille's saccharine-sweet question barely registered with my kiss-muffled brain.

If he could do that with just one tiny kiss, what else could that mouth do?

Iker stared down at me, his eyes boring into mine with a touch of confusion and something else that—

"Langley!" Camille snapped.

I blinked, bracing my hands on Iker's arms as I looked to find her standing next to us now. "I'm sorry?"

"The reservations?" she reminded me, her eyes narrowing just a fraction.

"Oh, right. Yeah, I got them moved like you wanted. No problem. Even updated the board and everything!" I smiled at her in an open dare.

"Hmm. Thanks." Her attention darted toward Iker and back to me, as if she'd heard me stake my claim—and the challenge in my voice—loud and clear.

I wasn't going to let this on go without a fight.

"Well then, let's not keep everyone waiting. There's a backyard barbecue to get to!" She crinkled her nose with a little grin.

"We'll be there in a second," Iker said, his low, growling voice rumbling against my breasts...because I was still pressed tightly against his chest.

And his eyes were still on me. Only me.

Oh.

"Everyone's waiting," Camille sang.

"This will only take a minute. We'll be right out," Iker replied as his gaze dropped to my lips.

"Huh. Right, then, okay." She walked away from our little moment, if the sound of her heels was any indication. I was too busy looking at Iker to watch.

"Sorry," I whispered as he turned me in the hallway.

"Really?" His eyebrows shot up with his nearly silent reply.

I caught the retreating blur of white pause in my peripheral. Great, Camille was waiting at the end of the hallway, no doubt listening.

My voice dropped even softer. "I didn't think, just... reacted, and—"

My back met the wall as his mouth covered mine.

There was no tentative, tender brushing of lips. No apology. I opened under him and his tongue rubbed against mine, sliding into my mouth like he owned it.

Maybe he did and I hadn't even been aware of it until right then.

His hands framed my face as he kissed me deeper, tasting like the wintergreen mints he'd left in my car yesterday. He stole my breath, my reason, and my inhibitions with every stroke of his tongue, until I was kissing him back just as fiercely, winding my arms around his neck.

Pure want slammed into me, filling every cell in my body that came into contact with Iker. It was more than chemistry. It felt...necessary, like air, or water.

He didn't kiss me like he was being forced to, or even like he wanted to. He kissed me like he *needed* to. When a sound like a whimper slipped from my lips, I felt him shift. I was lifted to the very tips of my toes and suddenly we were eye level with one another.

His coarse, super-short hair tickled my palms as I held the back of his head and leaned into his kiss. The world didn't narrow to Iker, there was simply nothing outside of him—outside of this moment.

"Langley," he whispered before pressing me harder against the wall, until all I felt was him.

All I ever wanted to feel was him.

I pulled him back to my mouth and he took it, kissing me breathless for another exquisite moment.

The kiss stopped as suddenly as it had started.

"She's gone," he said, leaning his forehead on mine. His voice was low, sandpaper-rough.

"Oh," I replied, my senses coming back to me.

He retreated, and I realized why I could look him straight in the eye. My ass was supported by his hands, and my feet were nowhere near the ground.

If my dress had allowed it, I probably would have had my legs wrapped around his damn waist. Luckily, the very expensive and form-fitting fabric had kept my thighs good and locked together.

He lowered me slowly, sending a whole new batch of tingles racing through my nerve-endings as I rubbed against every hard line of him on the way down.

It had all been for show, right?

"She was watching," he confirmed my thought as my feet reached the floor.

"Oh," I repeated. Because even though my body had stopped, my brain was still kissing him.

He stepped back, breaking our physical connection.

"I didn't think," he said with a shake of his head, giving my earlier words back to me. "Just...reacted."

A sense of loss swept over me, which was just downright stupid because he was never mine to lose. It was perilous to my foolish heart to even begin to think like that.

"And I don't regret it," he finished, as if he'd been speaking to himself, not me.

With this admission, that sense of loss was replaced with something even more dangerous—longing.

Before I could overthink any of it, he took my hand and I led him through the hallway and past the kitchen, and finally through the French doors at the terrace.

"This is not a barbecue," he muttered as he surveyed the lawn.

I took in the half-dozen banquet tables covered with food, including one with a tiered display of macarons, and the guests that milled about on the patio just below us.

"What would you call it?" I asked him as just about every head turned toward us.

"Ridiculous," he answered. "I would call it ridiculous and pretentious."

I laughed as he walked me down the stone steps to join the party of about six dozen people. *Only the closest of friends and family,* Camille had promised.

Virginia gave me a smile that didn't reach her eyes as she clanged something against her wine glass. "Well, now that we're finally all here," she began, turning to where Camille stood, leaning into Richard with her arm wrapped around her waist.

Dad winked at me from Virginia's side, and I gave him my first genuine smile of the party.

"I just want to thank you all for coming today," Virginia said, her voice thick with forced emotion. "It means so much to us to see our beloved daughter marry the love of her life."

Iker's hand tightened around mine, no doubt in response to Virginia's words.

I squeezed him twice, letting him know I was okay. This was nothing new in my world. I'd long ago learned to fake it when it came to any true emotions in dealing with them.

"Waiters?" Virginia ordered with a crook of her fingers.

White-jacketed staff came forward, all holding trays of charged champagne flutes. Iker took one and handed it to me before securing one for himself, never letting go of my hand.

"If you'll all raise your glasses," Virginia requested, lifting hers.

I did as she asked, noticing Iker kept his low and loose in his hand.

"To Camille and Richard. May your life be filled with all the love and happiness you both so richly deserve." Genuine tears filled Virginia's eyes.

There it was again, that ache from the empty place in my life where Mom should have been.

"To Camille and Richard," the crowd responded appropriately. I sipped my champagne at the same time we all did, completing the toast as Camille looked up at Richard dotingly.

"They certainly deserve each other," Iker muttered.

I sputtered, nearly sending wine out of my nose.

"Are you okay?" Iker asked, grinning down at me as the crowd headed for the tables.

I laughed in response, covering my mouth with the heel of my hand...that happened to still be holding my champagne flute. It tipped, sending the clear, sweet liquid straight to the patio.

"It's good to see you laugh," Dad said, barely dodging the deluge as it splashed toward his shoes.

"It's nice to be laughing," I admitted, as he leaned in and kissed my cheek. "Dad, this is Iker Alvarez. Iker, this is my dad, Corbin Vaughn."

Iker let go of me, but only to swap his glass so he could shake my dad's hand. "Sir," he said, his voice strong and sure, "you have a lovely home, but an even lovelier daughter."

Holy smooth-talker, Batman.

"So very true, though I can't take credit. Langley is her mother, through and through," Dad responded, smiling at Iker. "I'm glad to meet the man who makes her smile."

"Likewise."

Handshake over, the two men both looked at me.

I was out of words. What exactly was a girl supposed to say after she introduced her very real, very heartfelt dad to her very fake boyfriend?

"This is some party," Iker filled the silence for me.

"It's"—Dad sighed—"a little over the top."

I flat-out snort-laughed, earning me a real laugh from Dad.

"You know it, I know it, and I'm pretty sure even Virginia knows it. But it makes her happy, so here we have it." He gestured to the guests who were making their way through the buffet.

"It's definitely not what I was expecting when Langley told me you were having a barbecue," Iker admitted.

"Oh? You pictured her dad in an apron, flipping burgers, while a few guests grabbed beers from a cooler?" Dad asked.

"Something like that."

"Yeah, me too." Dad shook his head with a wry grin. "But I guess anything can be called a barbecue as long as that's what you're serving, right?"

"Darling!" Virginia called out from where she was holding court, Camille at her side.

"And...I've been summoned. You two have a...good... or at least passable time. I'll be...over there. Catch up later?" he asked.

"Definitely," I assured him.

"I like him," Iker said softly as Dad walked away.

"You sound surprised." I looked up at him, squinting against the sun.

"I am. I expected him to be an uptight asshole."

I laughed again. Man, I had to watch it, or I was going to get way too used to the feeling. Then I'd miss it all the more when he left. "There's only room for two of those in our family," I answered, motioning toward Virginia and Camille.

"And these?" he asked, his voice dropping as the bridal party came toward us.

"These are much, much worse," I answered before plastering a smile on my face. "Hi, guys."

"Langley!" Sophie Anders squealed, and wrapped me in a hug. "It's been forever since we've seen you!"

Because I had successfully avoided everyone in this group like the bubonic plague. They'd all known about Richard and Camille, and none of them—not one single, so-called friend—had told me the truth. They'd waited for me to stumble onto it myself.

In my own bed.

No doubt because Camille had needed to check off that box on her bucket list.

"Where have you been hiding him?" Sophie asked as the group gathered around us. Five groomsmen. Five bridesmaids.

All of us had gone to school together, known one another for at least a decade, and yet I felt closer to Iker in the few days I'd known him than I did any of them.

The grueling task of introductions and small talk began, and Iker handled dozens of questions with the same upfront, no-nonsense tone I'd learned to expect from him.

Once the subject turned to the perfection of the upcoming marriage, and my spine had stiffened enough to support the damned house we were outside of, Iker took my cue and declared he was hungry, and we excused ourselves.

"Thank you," I told him as we headed for the buffet.

"No problem. I'm not really big on crowds anyway. There might not be a lot of people here, but they sure like to stand way too close."

A few minutes and full plates later, we removed ourselves from the crowd, sitting on the double swing at the far corner of the yard. I set my plate on the side table, kicked off my heels and tucked my feet under me, resting my head against the tall, wooden back of the swing.

"I like you like this." Iker broke the comfortable silence.

"Like what?" I rolled my head along the back of the swing to look at him. "Barefoot and swinging?"

"Yeah. Like...you." He put his plate down on the stone table next to his side of the swing, then reached for my legs, pulling my feet into his lap. "Whoever that was over there with those people..." He shook his head. "I'm not a fan. I can't even see the real you under those fake-ass smiles and phony laughs."

"Good. Then my impenetrable armor is working."

"More armor?"

"I don't have a tux, just a different type of arsenal at my disposal," I teased, but stopped as I realized he wasn't joking. "They can't hurt me if they don't really know me, ya know."

He didn't respond, just studied me.

I looked away. Sometimes that intensity he had about him was just too much to have completely focused on me. Except when he was kissing me, that was.

"Did you fight for him? When you found out about them," he clarified, like I even needed the explanation.

I shook my head.

"Why?" He rested the palm of his hand on my shin.

A million different reasons went through my head.

"When she first moved in, I wanted a truce. I tried so hard to be her sister, and when it was obvious that was never going to happen, I attempted to be friends." I watched the movement of our little crowd, appreciating the twenty yards of grass that gave me enough separation from them to speak honestly. "She always dangled the possibility of some type of camaraderie in front of me, and it was usually right before she asked to borrow something."

"Yeah, I can see that."

"I always gave in, because I was a sucker for the dream family. The possibility of what I used to have with my own mom."

He squeezed my leg lightly.

"One by one, she would hand the things she'd borrowed back, but they'd be broken. Curling irons, a favorite pair of boots, an empty tube of lip gloss..." I sighed. "The list is probably about a bajillion miles long."

I reached up and let my fingers trail down the lavender chain that suspended the matching lavender swing. "This swing was my mother's."

His forehead wrinkled as his eyes narrowed, probably guessing where I was headed.

"It was her favorite place to read, and she loved this color. She never really cared about what things were *supposed* to be like. Only what they actually felt like, and she said this color made her feel like Saturday morning."

"Saturday morning." He spoke slowly, raising his eyebrows.

"Like sleeping in, getting the break you needed from the rest of the week."

He nodded.

"So, about a year after they moved in, Virginia started replacing everything my mother had decorated the house with, and Camille jumped right on board. I didn't really say anything about it. She was making Dad happy, and I wanted that for him. But when Camille said the swing was ugly and it needed to go, I finally spoke up."

"And you won," he assumed, glancing at the swing.

"Eventually. We were going to school one morning, and as we pulled out of the driveway, I saw the trash had been pulled to the curb, which was normal. But the swing was next to the cans. It was broken along the arms."

He looked at the intact arms of the swing, and then back to me.

"I hauled it to the garden shed, where they never went, and then I had it repaired and rehung, but I didn't say a word. Neither did Camille. A month later, I found it splattered in the same orange paint she'd done an art project in."

"You repainted it," he guessed.

I nodded. "I realized something. Camille could only take—only break—what I let her. She only had—only has—the power I give."

"And you gave him?"

"Would you stay with someone you knew would sleep with someone else? Who wouldn't give you honesty? Fidelity? Loyalty?"

His hand began stroking my leg in a lazy, comforting way. The brush of his thumb along the inside of my knee had my heart spinning in circles inside my chest.

"Hell no. What's mine is mine. I don't share, and I don't fucking forgive betrayal." He smirked at me. "I can be incredibly stingy and possessive. When you grow up with nothing, you tend to hold onto the things you treasure with both hands."

I looked over to where Richard's hand had strayed to the back of another one of my so-called friends. "Exactly. I didn't fight because I didn't want him after that, and honestly, he didn't want to be fought *for*. I respect myself a little too much to chase someone who doesn't want me. That relationship wasn't reparable."

We sat there in the quiet for a few minutes, swaying on my mom's lavender swing.

"You fought for me," he finally said, that gravelly tone sending shocks of awareness from his fingers caressing my leg all the way to my scalp. "In the hallway, when you kissed me. You fought for me."

I smiled and told myself to shrug it off. That kiss didn't mean the same thing to him as it did to me. "Yeah, I guess I did."

"Why?"

The unspoken hung between us. Why him? Why would I fight for a man I'd only known a few days when I didn't so much as scream at Richard?

"Because I see you, too. And you're not broken. Not like they all are." I nodded toward the patio. "You're…" I sighed, unable to come up with an adequate description.

"I'm what? Different? Real? Working-class?" He shook his head with a self-deprecating smile. "I'm completely broken and jagged in ways you don't know, and couldn't understand even if you wanted to, Langley."

I swallowed and met his stare head-on.

"Maybe," I admitted. Then I sucked in a deep breath and went for it, because why the hell not? I had nothing to lose. "But you seem like someone who would fight for me—who *did* fight for me—and I haven't really had that since my mother died. The least I could do was return the favor."

Because no matter how different we were, or the numerous financial trappings that separated us…he'd proven he was someone worth fighting for time and time again.

Chapter 6

Iker

"Are you sure this is what you want to do with your only free day this week? I'm sure you have better things to do with your time."

Langley sounded doubtful. Just like she had when I called her and asked her if she wanted to do something fun to blow off steam after that train wreck of a barbeque. Today was the only day neither one of us were scheduled within an inch of our lives, so after I finished up a few things I had to take care of at the base, and talked to Gael for a little bit, I found myself at loose ends and restless. My brother was pissed I wasn't spending this important week at home with him and our grandmother, and I couldn't blame him. I also wasn't ready to tell him the exact reason why I didn't make it home. I simply reassured him that it involved making sure he had the money for college.

There was no denying I wanted to see Langley outside of her prim and proper surroundings. I liked her best when she wasn't hiding behind the plastic shell she wore around her family and friends. I understood she wore that fake smile and air of disinterest for protection, but I hated it. Hated that the sweet, charming girl she was when she was alone with me, was suffocated and stifled because she was surrounded by money and mind-numbing obligations while being alienated in that big house.

Langley was clearly reluctant to accept my offer to bust free of the wedding madness for a few hours. I didn't think it had anything to do with her not wanting to see me, but more with her not wanting to come across as an imposition. We'd practically been in each other's pocket the last few days and I knew I'd seen pretty much every secret her wealthy family went out of their way to hide from the rest of the world. So, it took a little convincing and a promise that where we were going was guaranteed to alleviate some of her stress to get her to agree to spend the afternoon with me. At the end of the call, I swore I'd never had to work so hard for a date...real or fake. Usually, all I had to do was flash the dimple and let a little bit of my drawl loose and a date with whomever was a sure thing. Nothing about Langley was that easy. Which may have been why I couldn't stop thinking about her...or that rushed kiss.

"I took care of work stuff early this morning. If the rehearsal dinner is going to be anything like that barbeque, I think it will do us both a world of good to blow off some steam beforehand." Plus, there was a clock counting down in the back of my head. Time was running out, quickly, on the opportunities I had for frivolous fun...and to enjoy having her in my life.

Slowly, Langley nodded. I wasn't prepared for the impact her blindingly white and bright smile was going to have on my insides when she turned it my way. My heart literally squeezed, and all the air in my lungs froze at her open and unguarded expression.

"When you said we were going to shoot stuff, this isn't what I pictured. Not at all."

I looked at the giant warehouse housing the laser tag course and grinned. "Real weapons are part of my everyday reality. I wanted to play today." So was having to use them to protect my country. I had no desire to spend my free time at the shooting range when I was there for work all the time. But, I was pretty sure Langley had never had the opportunity to run around the course like a lunatic, dodging the electric shots and aiming for the sensors on the opponents' vests. It would be fun to see how the sorority girl handled hunting, as well as being the hunted. Underneath her polished veneer, she had threads of steel running throughout. She had to be tough in order to put up with her stepmother and sister's blatant machinations.

I'd watched it play out all day yesterday. In front of Corbin Vaughn, Camille and Virginia played sweet as could be. They treated Langley like part of the family. They included her, even fawned over her to the point of absurdity, but as soon as the man's back was turned or his attention was elsewhere, they came at Langley with claws drawn and teeth bared.

I couldn't understand how her father couldn't see what was going on, and it annoyed me Langley went to just as many lengths to keep the reality of her relationship with her dad's wife and new family hidden. I understood she wanted to shield him from what she was going through, but the man should be protecting his daughter, not the other way around. It irritated me even more when Camille and Virginia tag-teamed Langley. Two against one was bullshit, but my fake-girlfriend tolerated it with an even faker smile.

I climbed out of the truck and made my way to the passenger side so I could get the door for my very pretty date. Since today had nothing to do with putting a wrench in her stepsister's wedding, and I was the one who asked her out, I was treating it as a real date. Langley didn't need to know that, though. The chances of someone like her really going out with someone like me were slim to none. I was going to take what I could get, and be thankful she felt like she owed me for the time being.

I nearly swallowed my tongue when her long, bare legs swung out the door. She was definitely on the short side, but that didn't stop her from having really nice legs. She was wearing a pair of tiny denim shorts with white lace along the hem and around the pockets, and a pair of white Adidas. She also had on a white tank top with little yellow flowers all over it. It was the most dressed down I'd ever seen her, and I liked it. Without the dresses and high heels, she seemed much more approachable and accessible.

Her glossy ponytail bounced slightly when she landed on the ground in front of me. I reached out a hand to steady her, and told myself I could absolutely *not* pull her closer and hold her tight. Instead, I inhaled the slightly floral scent wafting from her hair and grabbed her hand.

"Let's go kick some laser tag butt."

"Have you done this before?" She sounded out of breath, so I slowed my pace to match her shorter stride.

"A couple of times. I've taken Gael and a couple of his buddies, and I had a guy in my unit who decided laser tag would be a fun bachelor party idea."

I had no idea how someone as fun as Langley dealt with all those unspoken rules and proper standards all the time. It was like living under a particularly finicky microscope. I bumped her shoulder with mine and told her softly, "Sometimes dark places and sudden flashes of light aren't the best for me. I'm a pretty well-adjusted dude, but you know"—I shrugged—"it's hard to fight your own mind."

"Have you...always struggled with that?" Her eyes softened.

"No, but a year in Afghanistan changed a few things. None of them really for the better."

She didn't press, just waited patiently for me to continue, so I did.

"I get jumpy with loud noises," I admitted. "My head knows I'm stateside, but my body forgets sometimes. That whole fight-or-flight thing kicks in."

"You don't seem like a flight kind of guy."

"Exactly." A wry smile twisted my lips. "Which put me in a lot of those loud-noise situations while I was deployed."

I heard her suck in a breath, and a moment later, she used the hold I had on her hand to pull me to a jerky stop. "Let's go do something else."

See, she was so damn sweet. And considerate. She barely knew me and she was worried about me. Worried about how I might react to something that might make me uncomfortable. No one, aside from my small family, had cared about my comfort and mental well-being in a long time.

"It's fine. I wouldn't have suggested this if I wasn't up for it." I watched as she considered me carefully for a full minute. Eventually, she must've decided I knew my own limits and slowly started walking toward the entrance again. I took the opportunity to follow behind her, enjoying the way her delicate and subtle curves filled out those short jean shorts.

Once we got inside the building and signed in, the staff put us with a group of teenagers who were all obviously on dates. They were arguing about how to split up the teams, when one of the guys, obviously the leader of the bunch, suggested we split into boys versus girls. The teen girls looked horrified by the suggestion, but Langley pointed at me, blue eyes glittering with mirth and challenge, and muttered, "You're going down, soldier boy."

I chuckled and arched an eyebrow. "Bring it on, baby." Her brash confidence was sexy as hell. I only wished she felt free enough to show it when she was dealing with those witches in her house.

We strapped on the gear and took our laser guns, entering the dark, glow-in-the-dark course, one at a time. A couple of the teenage boys looked at me, a couple of the others looked toward the mouthy leader. Since sending the girls off on their own was his idea, this could be his show. I'd been around enough assholes in the military who were exactly like him, so I knew to steer clear of this tool. He was obviously the type who didn't take to losing well, and this game was supposed to be fun.

"Let's stay on the outside of the course and try and push all the girls toward the center. We can pick them off one by one." He gave me a look and I just shrugged in response. I took orders for a living, but when I was off the clock, I tended to do whatever the hell I wanted. I'd never quite shaken my youthful rebellion. And there was no way this little punk was anyone I would ever willingly listen to.

"Don't think my girl is stupid enough to fall for that, chief." I started to make my way to the first glowing barrier, and caught a flash of blonde hair zipping by out of the corner of my eye. She wasn't really mine, but damn if it didn't feel good to claim her in some kind of way, even for a short amount of time.

"Chicks always stick together. They even go to the bathroom together. If we corner one, the rest will follow." He sounded so sure of himself. It was going to be really fun to watch him get taken down a peg or two—by females, no less. He had no clue Langley was a wolf looking for prey, not a rabbit, waiting to be picked off.

Deciding to play along for the time being, I obediently split off with the rest of the boys, sticking to the outside part of the arena. I didn't see the girls anywhere, but a few moments later, a female shriek echoed out of the darkness and one of the boys called out, "Holly?"

The concern in his tone was obvious, and I wasn't surprised at all when he broke formation and darted in the direction of the scream. A second later, the red flashing lights indicated a member of our team had been hit. The girls scored their first point.

I heard the mouthy teenager swear and couldn't hold back my chuckle. It never paid to underestimate the fairer sex. They were tricky and far more diabolical than many gave them credit for. Let's face it, any adult male has a pretty good idea that women are often the stronger, savvier sex. These wet-behind-the-ears rookies were about to get their asses handed to them on one of Langley's silver platters.

A few minutes later, a blue light flashed overhead, indicating one of the boys had scored a point.

"Mark? Is that you? It's so dark in here." Another female voice whispered out of the darkness, and I felt my eyebrows raise. This plan was different than the fake scream of pain. This one was all about seduction. "I can barely see my hand in front of my face. Why aren't you saying anything? It better be you groping me."

"What? Jenna, get away from whoever that is. It isn't me." A second later, one of the teen boys bolted in front of the low wall I was crouched behind and was immediately taken out. The cheer from the girls that went up made me smile. They were crafty and I had no doubt who the mastermind behind this diabolical plan was.

"You guys are so stupid." The angry voice of the ringleader echoed through the darkness. "We can play those games too. Meghan, if you don't come out where I can see you right now, I'm going to break up with you."

What a douchebag move.

"What?" A female shriek followed the announcement. I heard hushed whispers and soft crying. "That's so mean, Jeremy."

"Whatever. I came to win. Come out now, or we're through."

Sighing, I pushed up from my hiding spot. I was tall enough I made an easy target. "Stop being a dick to your girlfriend, man. It's just a game."

"Get the fuck down. What's wrong with you?" I hated guys like him, and I felt really bad for his girlfriend. "Who says that kind of shit to their girlfriend? I hope she stays hidden until the very end and you do break up with her, so she can find herself a decent guy to date."

"Fuck you!"

It was no surprise when the kid gave up his hiding place and charged at me. A split-second later, the blue lights shrilled overhead and both our vests flashed, indicating we'd been hit. Overhead, an electronic siren sounded and declared the red team as the winners. The girls cheered and Langley appeared from behind one of the walls with her arm wrapped around a crying, redheaded teenage girl. The younger girl was cute. She could definitely do better than the asshole currently glaring at me with the fiery hatred of a thousand suns.

"You threw the game on purpose, asshole." The accusation wasn't wrong.

I lifted my eyebrows at him and nodded in the direction of the girls—Langley, specifically. "She is more important than any win. I didn't throw the game, I sacrificed myself because there is no way if it came down to just me and her at the end, I could take her out. She was going to win, no matter what."

He scoffed. "Pussy."

I rolled my eyes. "Yeah, yeah, yeah." As insults went, it was weak and not worth a reaction.

The redhead girl still cowering behind Langley suddenly sniffed loudly and took a step forward. I was happy to see her friends immediately surrounding her for support.

"You don't have to worry about breaking up with me, Jeremy. Because I'm breaking up with you. You're such a jerk." She flipped her hair over her shoulder in a very sassy way and turned on her heel.

"Wait. Meghan, don't do this. I'm sorry." The jerk wasn't so full of himself when faced with being dumped in front of his squad. Suddenly, the room was full of teenage boys trying to appease their girlfriends.

Laughing under my breath, I watched as Langley made her way to where I was standing, a small smile playing across her face.

"You didn't have to do that. I had a plan in place to win fair and square." She tapped a finger on the still-flashing light on my chest.

"Eh. I wanted to shoot him myself. Figured you doing it was the next best thing. I don't remember relationships being so complicated when I was that age." I took her gun from her and complimented her on her strategic skills. She flipped her hair over her shoulder, in similar fashion to Meghan, and started walking back to the front as I chuckled at her sass, while ogling her ass in those short-shorts.

We turned all the gear back in and headed to the parking lot. I asked her if she wanted to grab an early dinner somewhere, and ordered the bubble of delight in my chest to chill out when she agreed. That fragile thing was going to burst any day now, so it needed to stop getting bigger and bigger every time we were together.

"Do you date a lot?" The quiet question caught me off guard. When I told her everything was about me was an open book, and I was proud of where I came from, that didn't necessarily include my pretty lackadaisical approach toward women most of my life.

I'd always been so busy, loaded down with so many responsibilities, that starting something serious with anyone had never even crossed my mind. I liked women...*a lot*. But, I'd never found one I wanted to hold onto for longer than a few hours, until her.

"I date here and there. Since I answer to the army first and foremost, and never really know where I'm going to end up since I've been transferred so frequently, I tend to keep my options open. I always figured it was better to keep things casual than be responsible for someone else's broken heart. How about you? Aside from Richard, did you date much?"

She shook her head, which sent her long ponytail swinging. This time, I couldn't resist the urge to catch the shiny gold strands. I caught the ends of her ponytail and wrapped my fingers through the shiny locks. They slid across my fingers like silk.

Langley cocked her head to the side and wrinkled her nose cutely. "My dad was pretty strict. And then my mom got sick. Richard was really my first. He was very persistent." She looked up at me and flashed that grin, which always turned my insides to mush. "However, this has been the best date I've ever been on. Even if it wasn't a real one. I always have fun with you, even when everyone else around us is being awful. How do you make that happen?"

Maybe because the rest of the world faded away for her just like it did for me when we were together.

Letting go of her hair, I put my hand on her lower back and stepped into her, moving her backward until her spine was pressed up against the driver's side door of my truck. Her eyes widened and I watched as her throat moved up and down in a gulp as she tilted her head back to meet my gaze. Her palms hit my chest, and she made a soft sound which had everything behind the zipper on my jeans pulling tight.

"We weren't putting on a show for anyone today. There was no one to impress or rattle. It was just me and you, Langley. Who says this wasn't a real date?"

"Oh..." She exhaled a long, soft breath that feathered across my throat.

I dropped my head so I could drag the tip of my nose along the elegant arch of her high cheekbone. Her skin might've been the softest thing I'd ever touched in my life.

"If I kiss you right now, it isn't for any other reason than I really want to kiss you. How do you feel about that?" My voice was raspy and slightly uneven. Things were so convoluted between us, the lines between real and fake getting continually blurrier. There were still so many things she needed to know about me, about who I was and what I had to do.

But none of that mattered when she slowly licked her lips and whispered, "I feel like I might die if you don't kiss me for real."

She surprised a laugh out of me. I lifted my hand and rubbed my thumb along the line of her jaw. "Can't have that, can we?"

This kiss was different from the ones before.

I wasn't trying to prove a point. I wasn't being watched. I wasn't thinking about all the ways it was wrong, and instead was focused on everything about it that was so right.

She fit against me so perfectly. Every dip and curve lined up with all my hard and suddenly aching places.

Her arms wound around my neck as mine glided down her back and rested right above the back pockets on her shorts. I tugged her closer at the same time as I dropped my mouth over hers. I caught her soft sigh, and answered with a low growl.

When one of her bare legs lifted and wrapped around me, I stopped playing around and kissed her like we *both* might die if we didn't learn the way the other tasted.

She opened her lips when I flicked my tongue across the seam, asking for entrance. She tasted like peppermint, and the interior of her mouth was a slick, sexy inferno. She was hot, all over, and getting hotter the closer I pulled her and the deeper I kissed her.

I was under the mistaken impression she would be refined and slightly regal in a situation like this, but she returned the kiss as down and dirty as I gave it to her. She didn't hesitate to rub her tongue along mine, and I felt the sharp edge of her teeth more than once. Her nails dragged through the very short hair at the back of my head and if I wasn't mistaken, she rolled her hips against mine in a way that was more appropriate for a darkened room than a parking lot in the middle of the day.

It didn't surprise me she had a lot of fire hidden underneath the block of ice she kept her emotions frozen inside of. I'd seen a hint of the flames flickering at her edges every single time we were together.

I traced the full swell of her bottom lip with the tip of my tongue, and felt the way her nipples suddenly dug into my chest through the thin material of her tank top. I was a guy used to moving fast because there never seemed to be enough time to savor the good things in life, but Langley was about to push me from zero to full throttle in a matter of seconds. It was the wrong time and definitely the wrong place for that.

I pulled back slightly, taking my hands off her ass and clasping her blushing cheeks. She had a hot pink flush all across her chest that was now climbing up her neck, and her eyes looked dazed and slightly out of focus. It was a good look on her, and there was no denying the shot of pride that rushed through my veins at being the one who put it there.

"Full of surprises, aren't you, Langley Vaughn?" Her tongue darted out again and swept across her damp lower lip. She made a face, and I was pretty sure she was tasting me and enjoying it. She was trying to kill me with every movement she made. I cleared my throat. "Let's get some food and I'll take you back to your castle before my truck turns into a pumpkin."

She nodded. Before she released her hold on me entirely, though, she braced her hands on my shoulders and lifted onto the toes of her sneakers so she could plant her lips firmly on the slight indent in my cheek. I felt my eyes widen in surprise as she grinned against the dimple she just kissed.

"I've wanted to do that since the first time you smiled at me."

I had no clue what I was doing with this girl anymore, or why she was the only one who so effortlessly slipped past years of hard-earned defenses. All I knew was the ten grand had stopped being the only reason I wanted to spend time with her long before her tailor groped me and her stepsister tried to kiss me.

Chapter 7

Langley

"It's really only for the sex, isn't it?" Camille asked, lifting a cucumber from her eyelid.

I felt the stare of every single bridesmaid as we reclined on the soft lounges in the spa, waiting for our next treatment.

"At least it looks like you'll have sun tomorrow for your wedding day," I noted, looking out of the floor-to-ceiling windows that offered an impeccable mountain view.

"No, really. Come on, Langley. We're all curious," Camille cajoled, her tone sliding into that sweet maliciousness I knew all-too-well.

"About the weather?" I smiled at Camille, and reached for my phone on the small table between us.

She snatched it away as my fingers grazed the case.

"Camille!" I snapped.

"What? You wouldn't deny me this little thing, would you, Langley?" She made her eyes go all soft as she dangled my phone.

"Deny you *what?* Last time I checked, you had everything you *wanted.*" My smile stayed far from my eyes, while my intent with my words hit the bullseye.

She dropped the pretense of being nice, and narrowed her eyes. "You know it can't really go anywhere between you two, right?"

"Cammy, be nice," Nessa chastised from Camille's other side.

"But I *am* being nice," she answered Nessa, while looking straight at me. "Would a good sister let you continue with this disastrous rebound? Let you think you had any kind of actual future with that guy?"

"Iker really isn't any of your concern, now is he?" I leaned over for my phone and she ripped it away again. "God, Camille, stop acting like you're five and give me my phone."

"He's nothing, Langley," she continued, her eyes glacial. "He's not in college. He has no manners to speak of, and doesn't fit in our world. And let's not even discuss all of those hideous tattoos he has. You two don't belong together. He came from nothing and he's going nowhere."

I stood, uncaring that my robe stayed closed only at the mercy of the terry cloth tie. "And yet, that didn't stop you from trying to hook up with him at the barbecue, did it?"

She hissed, her gaze darting over to where Virginia sat with Richard's mom, oblivious to the storm brewing across the room. "He's pretty. I'll give you that. So, go ahead and have your fun, *sis*. Just don't expect Daddy to sign over your trust fund with a leech like that standing by your side."

I blinked. *She doesn't know.* Of course she didn't. My trust fund hadn't been funded by my dad's money. It had come from the wealthier of my parents—my mother. She thought I was waiting—like she was—for my twenty-fifth birthday.

I wrestled my cell phone out of her hand, a quick glance telling me that Iker had texted a few minutes ago, no doubt sparking this whole conversation.

"Cat got your tongue?" Camille stretched on her chaise.

"Nope, I just stopped caring about what you think about me...and my life...five years ago, so..." I shrugged, dropping the compliant bridesmaid/sister act. If she wasn't pulling her punches, then neither was I.

"I think he's hot," Nessa said, flipping the page in her magazine.

"I second that," Phoebe chimed in behind me.

"Third," Zoe added.

Camille's bridesmaids obviously had good taste. He *was* hot. He was also smart, dedicated to his family, funny, and strong. There was much more to him beyond the sexy body and dark, bedroom eyes.

"I didn't say he wasn't hot," Camille snapped. "Just that he's obviously only here for your money, because someone who looks like that doesn't date someone who looks like..." She scanned me up and down. "You know. Without a good reason. Or millions of good reasons."

He's only here for your money.

My stomach hit the floor, because in a way, she was right. But somewhere between the parking lot that night, and laser tag yesterday, it had started to feel *real*.

Sure, I'd paid him to be here, but he wasn't the kind of guy to stick around for a trust-fund girl. Besides, it wasn't like he even knew how much money I had, or even knew about a trust fund.

"Are you ladies ready for your next treatment?" Mandy, the spa attendant, asked in that soothing, you're-supposed-to-be-all-zen-in-a-spa voice as she came over to our lounges.

"Absolutely! It's been just so perfect today!" Camille grinned up at the young woman as Virginia came over. "Right, Mom?"

"Yes, perfect," Virginia replied. "Perfect day for a perfect girl."

Oh, fucking kill me now.

I swiped my phone open to see Iker's text.

Iker: just got here.

Iker: found your dad.

He was early, and I was glad.

"Let's go, *sis*," Camille whispered in my ear. "I know the next treatment should help exfoliate all that dirt off you."

"You're just pissed because he made it clear he didn't want you," I said to her, my tone low as the others continued down the hall.

"I'm sorry?" She spun, putting her hands on her hips. "What makes you think I even offered?"

I ignored the question. There was no point arguing with a pathological liar. I'd witnessed her advance on Iker with my own two eyes and ears. And watched the way Iker coolly shut her down.

"He didn't want you. You couldn't take him and then use him to break me. So, you're trying to use the *idea* of him to scare me. But you don't know the first thing about him."

"I have no idea what you're talking about." She folded her arms across her chest.

"Girls!" Virginia sang. "We don't want to get behind schedule."

Camille stared at me in open challenge.

You promised Dad. It was the refrain that kept me going. It was also the only promise I'd made to him I really, really wanted to break.

"Why can't you just be happy?" My voice was so quiet even I barely heard it. "When is it ever going to be enough for you?"

"Girls." Virginia reached us, a smile on her face and ice in her eyes. "Now."

"Yeah, I think I'd rather not," I said slowly, testing out each word on my tongue. Iker was here, and if I could have a few hours alone with him before the madness of tonight, I was taking it.

Without another word, I left our little duck-line and walked straight to the locker room. I found the mahogany cabinet with my assigned number on it, and took my bag out, not pausing to put my clothes on before I headed for the elevator.

I had to get out of here. Now.

"Langley," Virginia hissed, power walking in my direction as the doors opened in front of me.

"Have fun! I'll see you later," I called out as the doors shut in her face.

An immediate stab of panic hit me as the elevator lowered me to the first floor of the golf club. She'd most definitely take this out on my dad.

The elevator *dinged*, and I walked out, my slippers catching on the navy blue and gold carpet as I walked down the hall. I'd slip out the side door and get to the suite, change, then find Iker.

"Langley?"

My head snapped up to see Iker standing in the foyer of the golf club, a small duffel bag in one hand and a garment bag draped over his shoulder.

"Hey! I thought you were with my dad?" I felt incredibly short as I stared up at him.

Because I was still in slippers from the spa.

He looked good enough to eat in black cargo shorts and a green polo.

"I was, but he paused my interrogation to set up the lie detector."

My jaw dropped.

"Relax, I'm kidding. We finished the lie detector about twenty minutes ago. He just ran into the pro shop for something and I didn't want to haul my stuff in, so I'm waiting out here. What are you doing?" His gaze swept over me.

Heat rose in my cheeks, realizing my robe hit mid-thigh. "I came to find you."

"In a robe."

"It appears so."

He grinned, that dimple popping in his cheek, and I resisted the urge to kiss it.

"Langley Vaughn, what do you think you're doing?"

Virginia snapped as she entered the lobby. She had changed into tan capris and a sleeveless polo in record time, but was obviously flustered.

"Hanging out with my boyfriend," I answered. "That's the best way for *me* to relax."

"You've upset Camille and I won't have it! Get your spoiled butt back up there and get your massage like the rest of the bridal party!"

"Rich people are so damn weird," Iker muttered behind me.

"I'd rather not," I answered, not even looking in her direction, voice as cool as hers for once.

"I don't give a good goddamn what you want!" She stomped her foot like the spoiled child she'd just accused me of being.

"Hey, don't speak to her like that." Iker stepped between us.

"Miss Vaughn," another voice joined at my right. John, the golf club manager, was forced to intervene. "I hate to intrude, but what you're wearing doesn't exactly meet our dress code."

I looked down at my robe. "Right, I was just headed to my room."

"You're headed to the spa!" Virginia countered.

"What's going on?" Dad asked, carrying a small bag from the pro shop.

"Sir, your daughter's attire..."

"I'm just going to take her to the room." Iker to the rescue once again.

"She's upset Cammy and I won't have it, Corbin!" Virginia looked like she was going to burst a blood vessel.

Dad's attention flickered between all three before settling on me. "Langley?"

"I'm headed to my room," I told him. I wasn't wavering, and I wasn't caving in to Virginia's ridiculous demands this time.

"She can't just walk out on the other bridesmaids. It's selfish, it's put Cammy into a tizzy, and it's going to stop right now!" Virginia whirled in my father's direction, face flushed and hands clenched.

Dad's head tilted just a fraction as he studied me and then his wife.

Guilt clogged my throat. I'd promised to make this weekend easy, to go with the flow on everything, and here I was, causing trouble out in the open. I always planned to break that promise, but I'd hoped to be more subtle about it and leave my hired date as the bad guy. But I wanted to be with Iker. And I wasn't walking away from ruffling Virginia's feathers for once. I wanted to smile, and laugh, and enjoy what time I had with my date, because he *wasn't* a bad guy. I was so sick of the spectacle surrounding Camille and this wedding.

"Sir, she really can't stay here dressed like this," John urged as a member came through the front doors, their eyebrows raising to the second floor.

I heard a zip, then felt the soft fabric of Iker's suit coat settle on my shoulders.

"That's hardly what I meant," John argued.

"Look, she's not in jeans and even has on a sport coat. I can throw a tie on her if that makes you feel better," Iker answered. The challenge in his dark eyes was clear, and John immediately backed down as my father snickered in amusement. I wouldn't want to go toe-to-toe with this man when he was in protective mode either.

All while Dad and I communicated wordlessly.

"Corbin!" Virginia pleaded, changing tactics. "Please, love. It's Cammy's day. Not Langley's."

I'd go back if Dad asked me to. I knew it and so did he. I would do anything to keep the peace for him. However, Iker made me realize it was time to expect my father to return the favor.

"*Tomorrow* is Camille's day," Dad corrected Virginia softly. "*Tomorrow*, she's marrying Langley's first love. Which you already know I take major issue with. I think *today* we can keep both our daughters' best interests at heart and give Langley the space she's asking for."

Until he mentioned it, I'd forgotten all about the fuss he'd put up when Virginia demanded he pay for the wedding. My father hadn't been happy when Camille announced her engagement to my ex, and was even less thrilled when he found out he was expected to foot the bill. Eventually, he caved, because he always did, but for a moment he'd still been my hero.

"I'll be at the rehearsal on time, with a smile. I promise." I nodded.

"I know you will, sweet pea." Dad flashed me a grin and gave Iker a look I couldn't quite decipher.

Virginia's mouth gaped. I'd never gone against her in front of my dad. I'd never won. But then again, I'd never tried. I'd never had a reason like I did now—Iker.

"Miss Vaughn," John begged.

"We're going right now," Iker told him, holding his duffel and garment bag in one hand, and ushering me out with his other on my lower back.

"You're killing me in that robe, by the way," he muttered as we found the elevator in the main hotel, earning more than a few stares from the five-star resort's guests.

"Embarrassed?' I asked as we rose to our floor.

"Turned on, actually," he admitted.

Before I could even begin to address that comment, the elevator *dinged* and we arrived at our floor. I opened the door to the suite and walked in, dropping my bag on the dining room table.

"So, this is ours. I can get you your own room, of course, but it's got plenty of space."

Iker looked around, taking in the dining area, sitting room, and bedroom. "Pretty sure this suite is bigger than my apartment."

"Do you live on base?" I asked, breaching the barrier of the real world.

"Not since I was an E-4. You could probably fit my old barracks in here about ten times over."

"So, you don't want your own room?" I asked.

He shook his head. "No, I don't want my own room. But now that you've escaped the clutches of your wicked stepmother, what would you like to do with your hard-earned"—he checked his watch—"four hours of freedom?"

I grinned. "Did you know there's a waterslide here?"

"Of course there is," he replied with a snort.

But without argument, he went with me after I changed and headed out to the pool.

Five hours later, we stood outside the chapel, Iker just behind me, getting our instructions on bubble blowing. Iker looked edible in his suit, even if he did tug at the tie and fiddle with the cufflinks every now and again.

"And as the bubbles rise, you'll exit like this," the wedding planner told Camille and Richard.

"You burnt your nose," Iker whispered, leaning down so his lips grazed my ear.

A shiver danced down my spine.

"Someone didn't want to leave the waterslide," I answered, turning slightly so my lips grazed the corner of his.

"If by someone, you mean *you*," he teased, "then *you* are correct."

"And this is where the horse-drawn carriage will wait." The wedding planner motioned toward the space right in front of the curb.

"Are you shitting me?" Iker laughed softly. "A horse-drawn carriage?"

"She wanted a legit Cinderella carriage, but Richard put his foot down," I told him.

"Oh, *that's* where he draws the line? At the Cinderella carriage?" He sounded baffled, and I bet he was telling himself he was never getting married if all brides were this ridiculous.

"Where would you draw it?" I wondered what he would be like when he loved someone. Would he compromise? Give in to the silly things? I would have bet he'd move heaven and earth to make the woman he loved happy, to show her exactly how he valued her.

I kind of hated that unknown woman on principle alone.

"I would have drawn it the first time Camille tried to kiss me, and steal me away from you," he answered. "Hell, I already drew it," he finished on a whisper.

Uncaring that we were in full view of the bridal party, I turned, my blue dress swishing above my knees, and planted a soft kiss on that flashing dimple of his. Kissing the little indent was going to be my new favorite hobby for as long as he let me get away with it.

"Okay, boys and girls! That concludes the rehearsal, so let's head over to the restaurant for dinner!" Richard called out, already swaying on the sidewalk, obviously a bit drunk.

While the bridesmaids had been at the spa, the groomsmen had spent all day drinking on the golf course.

We made our way to the west side of the resort, through the marble-floored lobby, and into the restaurant where a U-shaped table had been set, with the lake and main hotel as a backdrop.

Iker excused himself to take a phone call as our group disbursed to the bar that had been set up in the corner, the table, or in my case—the view at the window.

"You look good, Langley." Richard stood in the spot next to me, holding a beer. He sighed and took a less-than-appropriate look at my ass. "Really good."

"You look engaged to my stepsister, Richard," I answered. "And a little drunk."

His eyes had that buzzed, glazed look as he laughed, which came out as a half-scoff, half-hyena sound. "I'm not *married* yet."

"I'm not doing this with you," I replied, and turned away from the window, only to be caught in the death-glare of Virginia.

"Outside. Now." She snapped her fingers at me like I was a toy poodle, and exited.

I counted to three, trying to find even the smallest thread of patience, and then followed.

"What the hell did you think you were doing today?" she seethed, her hands in fists at her side.

"I thought we already had this discussion." And I had zero desire to have it again.

"Don't you dare sass me. Not today. You've already ruined enough!" Her gaze swung through the lobby, no doubt making sure we wouldn't be overheard.

"How did I ruin anything? I excused myself from a tense situation. If anything, the girls should have had a fabulous time without me, because let's be real, no one actually wants me here. It was a win-win for the entire bridal party, in my opinion." My stomach clenched with the effort it took to keep my voice calm and level.

"Listen. To. Me. I love your father, and I've done everything I can to make us a family. You fight me at every turn. You won't let go of your mother's things. You won't share your space, or your things, with Camille. Hell would freeze over before you'd willingly share your dad with her! I'm sorry she fell in love with your ex, and that he found her more appealing—"

"He wasn't my ex at the time," I whispered, unable to keep it in.

"Even now, you can't just let her be happy! I told Camille it was stupid to include you in the bridal party, that you would only be a jealous wretch, and look!" She waved her hand at me. "She wanted you to be her bridesmaid. She wanted you as a sister! You think it was so hard for you to lose your mother, and I'm sure it hurt, but Camille never even *knew* her father. Have you ever stopped to think about what your foolish, selfish actions have done to her? To me? To your father?"

She may as well have punched me in the gut.

"I think that's more than enough," Iker's voice came from behind me.

"Who gives a damn what you think?" Virginia retorted, then pushed past me as she headed back to the rehearsal dinner. "Get your ass back in here and smile, Langley. For once in your life, act like the lady your mother raised you to be."

My entire body tensed as I watched her stomp away, and even though logically I knew I was still the same height I'd been when I'd followed Virginia out, I felt about three feet tall.

"Here, I figured you might need this." Iker faced me and handed over a martini.

"How do you know what I drink?" I asked, my hand trembling as I reached for the glass.

"I watched you the night we met."

I ignored the response my heart gave to his admission, tipped the cool liquid to my lips, and then swallowed over and over until it was gone.

"Sorry about the phone call. Work stuff."

"On a Friday night?"

"The aarmy doesn't care if it's Friday night or Christmas morning. They call. You answer." He glanced toward the door and took a sip of his beer. "I hate when you let her talk to you like that."

"I don't *let* her do anything," I snapped back.

"Sure you do," he replied, with as much emotion as an iceberg. "Every time you don't dish it back to her like you just did to me. Every time you don't tell your dad what's really going on. Every time you fix a swing yourself instead of demanding one of them fix it. It's like you're okay with it, Langley. I just can't figure out why because that's not the woman I've spent the last week with."

My cheeks burned, anger swirling in my blood like acid, burning for an outlet.

"You think you know? Because what, we've known each other for a week? Because you've seen a sliver of my life, of what goes on behind closed doors?" My mouth took that anger and ran with it, and no matter how loudly my brain screamed, it couldn't catch up. "My dad went through hell when my mom died. Not just depression, Iker. *Hell.* It was like he'd lost his very soul, not just his soulmate. And when Virginia came around, even as awful as she is, she woke him up and he came back to me. So, if the cost for having him back is that I have to deal with... them, then I guess it's worth it."

His chiseled jaw flexed, and those warm, dark eyes turned obsidian.

"I do know because I've known you for a week. Because I can see from the outside of this fucking snow globe you call a life. I have something you don't—perspective on both the insanity of this shit, and the cage you willingly allow yourself to live in. And I'm telling you that you don't have to pay the price for your father's happiness. That man loves you. If he checked out when your mom died, I'm sorry, but he's here, now. And I can tell you that he would want to know how they treat you. I honestly believe he would protect you."

I ripped my eyes away from his, staring out the glass doors that led to the lake. I hated that he saw into me, saw through the gold-plated façade my family kept in place. Iker held up a mirror to my life and made me look, and it was painful, and inconvenient, and yet so necessary.

"Maybe she's right, though." I shook my head. "Maybe I should have shared more. Maybe holding onto my mother shoved Virginia away. Maybe—"

Iker cupped my cheek in his hand, drawing my gaze back to him.

"No," he said quietly. "You can't let the guilt in, or she wins. Don't give her another inch, Langley. She's already taken miles."

Iker's attention shifted to something—someone behind me.

"Hey, kids, we're getting started in here. Want to join us?" my dad asked.

"We'll be right in, sir." Iker nodded at Dad, then studied me. "Are you okay?"

I nodded. "Yeah. I'm sorry I yelled at you."

He grinned. "That was hardly yelling. I just wish you would put that anger where it belonged." He took my hand, and we walked into dinner, where everyone was already seated.

"Just let me know when you'd like me to set the tablecloth on fire," Iker whispered, kissing my cheek, then took his own chair beside me as dinner began.

He'd pulled out my chair, just like he'd opened my door during our date. Ugh, those butterflies were back in my stomach, and that awareness between us was only sharper.

I wanted him. The knowledge unsettled me more than that broken heel had. Wanting meant risk. Risk of rejection. Risk of embarrassment. It wasn't just a physical want, either—though the man had me keyed up simply by resting his hand on my thigh. I wanted...more from him. Wanted his blunt honesty, his perception, his simple presence in my life. I didn't want this weekend to end.

I watched him during dinner, making polite conversation with Phoebe, smiling when my dad cracked a joke down the table. His hand reached for mine often between courses, and he leaned over to kiss my cheek more than a few times, always whispering sarcastic suggestions on how to ruin the dinner.

Three courses in, he'd only had that single beer. The guys around us—the girls, too—had been putting them away with frequency, and it showed as Richard's dad stood, bringing the conversation to a halt.

"I just wanted to say thank you for coming tonight." He rubbed the bridge of his nose. "Richard, I'm just so proud of you and this step you're taking. Mom and I always knew you'd marry a good girl."

My back stiffened as the group laughed politely. Iker's hand found mine under the table, his fingers lacing tightly.

"No, really, Camille, you're everything we imagined for Richard. Beautiful, elegant, and intelligent. We're excited to welcome you into our family tomorrow. To Richard and Camille!"

Everyone raised their glasses, repeating the toast.

My lips parted, but the words wouldn't come.

"Now, enjoy the dessert bar!"

The party stood, and Iker tugged me to the window. "I'm glad he's marrying the girl who only acts good," he said, tipping my chin up.

"Yeah?" I forced a smile.

"Yeah." He lowered his face slowly, then brushed his lips over mine before kissing me sweetly, softly. "Because now I get to kiss you."

"Damn, get a room, you two," Richard slurred, more than wasted as he walked over to us.

I rolled my eyes at him. How funny that he'd been everything I thought I wanted, but now, standing here next to Iker, I couldn't imagine ever marrying Richard. The two didn't compare, not just physically, but in every other department.

"Congratulations, again," Iker said, but I saw the muscle in his neck flex.

"Yeah, I guess my gain is...your gain, too." He blatantly looked at me.

"Right. I'm sure glad you fell for Camille."

Richard didn't take his eyes off me. "Are you glad, Langley?" He swayed and threw his hand out to catch himself on the wall.

"You're drunk." I was pointing out the obvious.

"You've said that already tonight." He tried to smirk, but didn't pull it off. "So, Iker, what do you do in the army? I feel like I should know who I let in my family."

"We're not family," I snapped.

"Tomorrow, we will be," he said to me before swinging his head back to look at Iker. "So, what is it?"

"I'm a cav scout. Nineteen Delta." His arm wrapped around my waist, tucking me into his side. "First in, last out. That kind of thing."

It was clear Richard had no clue what any of the things Iker was saying meant.

"Kill anyone?"

I blanched, horrified. "Richard, what kind of question is that?"

"Come on, don't you want to know who you're fucking?" He threw out his other hand, sloshing liquor out of his glass. "I want to know."

"You get one warning," Iker cautioned, his voice level and low. All the scarier for it.

"Or you'll what? Don't you know who I am by now?" Richard's voice raised, which promptly sent every head swiveling in our direction.

"I don't really care who you are. I care how you speak to Langley."

"How I speak to Langley?" Richard laughed. "Oh, that's fucking perfect. I've known Langley since we were twelve. I know that girl inside and out. Can you say the same?" His brows lowered and he looked at me. "Can he, Langley? Does he know you like I do?"

"He knows me better." It was true. I'd shown more of myself to Iker in the last few days than I ever had to

Richard. Iker didn't need me to be perfect. Didn't need me as a showpiece or a trophy. Iker just needed me to be...me.

My eyes surveyed the room and landed on Camille. I sent her a pleading look.

She looked as stricken as I felt, and for the first time in my life...I felt bad for her.

"I highly doubt that. I can't figure out why you'd let this piece of trash touch you, when you could have your choice"—he swung his arm out again, losing the rest of the contents of his glass—"of guys from our...class, shall we say?"

"Ass, we shall say!" I snapped.

"You really are a dick, Dick," Iker responded, still cool and collected.

"Okay, honey, why don't we—" Camille tried, making her way over to us.

"Tell me, Langley, does he know about that little sound you make right before you come? Because—"

I blinked, and a moment later, Iker had Richard pinned against the wall.

"Oh, shit!" I heard one of the groomsmen shout.

Whoever wasn't looking our way sure as hell was now.

"I told you. One warning. You don't get to talk to her like that. Not now. Not ever. You gave up any right to her the minute you fucked her stepsister. Understand?" Iker's words seethed anger, low and quick, but the look Camille shot me said she'd heard them.

Richard's complexion ruddied as Iker pressed his arm against the base of his throat.

"Apologize."

Richard tried to push Iker off, but he wasn't strong enough.

"Apologize, *now*." The threat was there, plain as day. Iker did not come to play and he had lost any patience he may have had for Richard's bullshit not long after he met him.

Richard's eyes found mine. "I'm sorry."

Iker removed his arm and Richard sank to the floor.

Camille darted around Iker, dropping to her knees in her white silk sheath. "Baby!"

Iker sent one glare toward two of the slowly advancing groomsmen, and they backed away.

"I told you that he wouldn't fit in here!" Camille shrieked at me. "Look what you've done! This disaster is all your fault."

Iker held out his hand to me.

"Are you serious? Like she's going with you now," Richard spat.

Iker didn't flinch, didn't lower his hand, didn't say a single word.

He just waited for me to choose.

I could stay here, surrounded by what I knew, comfortable in my little cage, or I could take his hand and gain freedom.

The want came with the risk.

I stepped forward and took Iker's hand, strong and steady. As we left, I paused, looking down at Camille and Richard. "You guys have a great night. We'll see you tomorrow. Might want to sober him up a little, first. He says really stupid things when he's drunk and you don't want him to look hungover in your precious wedding photos."

Camille's jaw dropped, but I was too giddy to care.

I had Iker and my freedom.

I could finally breathe.

Rebellion felt almost as good on the inside as it looked on the outside.

Chapter 8

Iker

If I were someone else, someone who had enough money to pay for the damages, I would trash this hotel room. I was that pissed off.

It felt like everyone who had anything to do with this damn wedding took lessons in how to be exceptionally terrible, and I hated how Langley just accepted all the crap they were shoveling her way without question. I appreciated that the girl was willing to suffer in silence for her father—after all, I'd taken more than one hit in defense of my own family. But at some point, she had to realize enough was enough. It was her father's job to shield her, not the other way around. If she wasn't going to take the initiative to fill him in on how awful things were for her, I was going to have to find the time to have a chat with the man before I disappeared from her life for good. If anything, the phone call I'd taken from the L.T. right before dinner had driven that point home—I didn't belong in Langley's world.

I flinched when I felt Langley's hand rest on my tense shoulder as I paced angrily from one side of the hotel room to the other. The contact halted my jerky steps and I took a calming breath before meeting her concerned gaze.

"I feel like I should apologize, but I know I didn't do anything wrong. I knew everyone was going to be upset and judge you when I roped you into this. I had no idea it would be this bad, or that everyone was going to lose their damn minds."

She gasped when I caught her hand in mine and slowly backed her toward the massive bed in the center of the elegant hotel room. I grabbed her other hand and kept moving until the back of her knees hit the edge of the mattress. She went down without a fight, even as the position moved the hem of her dress up dangerously high on her smooth, tanned thighs. I kept both her hands trapped in one of mine as I leaned over her.

I traced the furrow between her pale eyebrows with my free hand, and ordered, "Don't you dare apologize for their bad behavior. Not now. Not ever."

She had been nothing but adorable and accepting since the night we met. She was the only thing keeping me from thinking all rich people had lost their damn minds.

Her blue eyes practically glowed as she stared up at me. The center of my chest throbbed painfully when her teeth suddenly bit down on her plump, lower lip.

"I won't apologize for them. Or for the fact that I'd rather spend time with you than pretending we're all one happy family. I'm not sure I would have survived this week without you, Iker. I don't know how to thank you for being here with me. I will be forever thankful I sat down next to you at the bar that night." A soft smile tugged at her lips, forcing me to bite back a groan.

She was stretched out beneath me like a very tempting buffet, and there was no way I could ignore the way all her soft and yielding parts lined up perfectly with the parts of my body that were getting harder and harder with each minute that passed.

"Your gratitude isn't at the top of the list of things I want from you at the moment, Langley." Surprisingly, neither was her money.

It was impossible to think of anything besides her velvety skin and slight curves when we were pressed together so tightly there wasn't even room for a deep breath between the two of us.

Her plush, pink lips twitched again, and this time I didn't bother to control the growl that rumbled out of my chest. I lowered my head so our foreheads touched and tried to convince myself the best thing for both of us would be for me to get up and walk away from her *right now*. Unfortunately, neither my dick nor my heart were exactly on board with that plan. In fact, it was the first time I could pinpoint both of those parts of my anatomy agreeing on one girl.

"What do you want?" Her tone was breathy and her eyes were making all kinds of dangerous promises. I wanted to take her up on them so badly I could taste it.

I wanted time.

More of it.

All of it.

But it was the one thing no one could give me, and the one thing I couldn't take for myself.

"Too many things to name, but I don't think what I want and what you need are the same thing." I was equally as conflicted as I was turned on.

Would it be fair to her to take things to the next level when the fact that she was paying me still lingered between us...and when she didn't really have a clue what being with me meant?

"What is it you think I need?" My entire body stiffened in response when her hands suddenly lifted and pushed the expensive suit jacket she bought for me off my shoulders. I had to let her hands go to shake the fabric loose, and I sucked in a breath when I felt her fingers on the buttons of my shirt.

I closed my eyes briefly and inhaled a sharp breath when she pulled the tails of the shirt from the waistband of my pants.

"You need someone who can protect you from half your family. Someone by your side who knows how to play these complicated, rich-people games. Someone who knows the rules. You've been going at it alone. You need someone who is on your side, indefinitely."

Permanence wasn't part of my game plan. However, she was the first woman who'd managed to make me wonder what it would be like to have someone special waiting for me. I always assumed leaving someone behind would feel like a burden and be a distraction. Langley made me question if my thinking had been selfish and backward this entire time. Maybe having someone to come home to would be comforting rather than suffocating...if that person was the *right* person.

My family missed me because they relied on me. They were used to me taking care of everyone and everything.

They missed me for other reasons as well, but we all knew I was the glue holding us together. Having someone like Langley waiting for my return meant I'd be coming back to someone looking forward to taking care of *me* for once. I'd always had to be strong, the one who never let the world see I was struggling. It felt different with Langley. I wondered if she would be able to put me back together if I came home shattered into a million pieces.

"You're wrong. I don't need someone to protect me. I needed someone to give me the strength to finally protect myself because, no matter what, I'm the one who has to fight this battle, day in and day out. I shouldn't rely on anyone else for that."

Her warm palms slid enticingly up my ribs underneath the fabric of my shirt, stopping briefly to trace the black roses inked high up on my side even though she couldn't see them. The tattooed thorns on the stems looked like they were digging into my skin and red drops of blood decorated my whole rib cage.

"Now ask me what I want, Iker." The challenge in her voice made my dick even harder than it already was.

Silently admitting defeat, I tugged the cufflinks that cost more than I made in a month off of the shirt and carelessly tossed them somewhere behind me.

"What do you want?" It was a useless question. I could see the answer in her eyes, and feel the answer in her delicate hands that held so much power over me right now.

She wanted me. Wanted this moment. Wanted the escape and the connection.

Instead of replying, one of her hands reached for the buckle of the Gucci belt she had bought for me, and the other reached for my face. I let her pull me back down so I was braced over her silk and lace-clad body. Her fingers were cool on my jaw, but her mouth was hot when our lips touched.

I liked the way she kissed. Liked that there was nothing pristine or polished about it.

It was a little desperate and hurried. It made me feel like she was just as impatient to get close as I was. It made me feel like she was just as caught up and helpless to fight this inexplicable connection we shared. When we kissed, when we touched, all the differences and contrasts in our lifestyles faded away. When our hands were on each other's bodies, the only thing that mattered was the way we made each other feel.

I steadied myself over her with an arm bent above her head. I let one of my knees slide between her parted legs, pushing the hem of her blue dress up even farther. Her fingers were quick with my belt and the zipper on my pants. The sound of it lowering was barely audible over our rapid breaths and the sound of my heart thundering in my ears.

My tongue circled hers as my free hand skated up the outside of her toned thigh. I felt her muscles quiver under the light touch and had to fight back a possessive growl. Making her react to my every caress, my every movement and sound, was highly addictive. I wanted to own all her quiet whimpers and gentle shakes. I wanted to claim the way she shuddered against me, and the way she pulled her mouth away from mine so she could gasp my name as my fingers found the lacy edge of her barely there panties. I wanted her to swear she wouldn't look at anyone else with those dazed baby-blues, and I wanted her to promise no other man would ever make her turn that enticing shade of pink. But I knew all of that was a pipe dream.

What I needed was to make the most of the time we did have together so regardless of what happened in the future, I knew she wouldn't be able to forget me. I might not be the right guy for her, but I definitely didn't mind being the guy she would compare every other man to in the future. I was okay being the right guy for her for the night.

Her lips skimmed across my jawline while her quick and clever hands went to work on getting me the rest of the way out of my shirt. I slipped my fingers under the elastic edge of her underwear and let out a surprised inhale against her wet, swollen mouth when my touch was met with damp, heated skin. She was soft and slippery. Hotter than hell, and so damn sexy. Her reactions were unguarded and unpracticed. Raw and so very real.

There was so much about us being together that was fake, it did something to my insides to know that at least when we were together like this, intimate and vulnerable, we could be entirely honest with one another. That knowledge spurred me on more than any amount of money ever could.

I deepened the kiss. Stealing her breath while trying to catch mine when I felt her body arch up off the bed, pressing her chest into mine and sending my exploring fingers closer and closer to the soft, sweet center of her body. I wanted to take my time. To savor the precious remaining seconds we had with each other. She was making it so damn hard, though. Every time she moved, the way she reached for me and held me close, pushed my self-control closer and closer to the breaking point.

I lifted my head so we could both catch a breath, and watched her with hooded eyes as her hands reached for the gaping fly of my pants and the visibly hard flesh behind the thin cotton of my black boxer-briefs. One of her legs shifted and I felt the heel of her stilettos dig into the back of my thigh. The sharp sting was almost enough to bring me back my senses, but just as the fog was about to clear, her long, elegant fingers brushed across the front of my underwear, making the straining erection behind the fabric kick in response.

"Stop thinking so hard." That smile she had, the one reserved only for me which rivaled the sun in brightness, claimed her kiss-reddened mouth. "Just feel. Everything."

Her knuckles continued to rub along the hard length of my cock, and I decided there was nothing I could do but take her advice because I was powerless against her allure.

I felt the way her hard nipples pressed into my bare chest.

I felt the way her wet, velvety folds fluttered when my fingers danced closer and closer to her heated center.

I felt the way her spine stiffened when I kissed and licked my way to her ear.

I felt the way her heart pounded and the way she shifted restlessly underneath me as my fingers finally found their way into the clasping warmth of her body.

We both moaned at the contact, and I nearly bit the tip of my tongue off when I felt her fingers slip into the stretchy fabric of my Calvins. Her palm was unbelievably soft when she fisted my painfully hard cock. My eyes slammed closed momentarily, and for the first time in a long time, I had to count backward in my mind to keep myself in check. I'd been so focused on her each and every reaction, each and every moan and shudder, I'd lost track of my own responses. I reacted to her just as quickly, and just as violently, as she did to me.

I muttered her name on a strangled breath when her fingers danced over the already leaking tip of my cock.

"Off." I was only capable of single syllables at the moment and I didn't have a free hand available to get the top of her dress down, so I ordered her to remove the barrier.

Langley's little shimmy and wiggle to get the blue fabric out of the way had her hand moving in an erratic rhythm up and down my rigid dick, but it was the sight of her small, high, rosy-tipped breasts that had me growling again. She was such a perfect, pretty handful. I couldn't wait to taste her…all over.

When I bent my head to drag my tongue across one puckered nipple, the motion pushed my fingers deeper inside her welcoming body. Her pussy clenched and fluttered around my fingers and she whimpered helplessly as I stroked her and sucked on her nipple at the same time. Her eyes fluttered closed and she whispered my name on a broken sigh, her hand finding its own distracting rhythm as we both tried our best to drive the other over the edge.

Not since high school had nothing more than the feel of a girl's hand wrapped tightly around my cock been enough to do me in. But, for some reason, Langley's mere touch was more than enough to have me hovering on the precipice of pure, unfiltered pleasure. I released the nipple I was torturing and dragged the very tip of my tongue across her chest to the other one. The sound she made when I pulled her other nipple into my mouth and used my teeth on the sensitive peak had uncontrollable heat coiling tightly at the base of my spine. The sensation caused the rest of my body to tighten and made my dick throb in Langley's tight grasp. When her thumb grazed the leaking slit again, I gasped against her breast and closed my eyes. For a second, I thought she was going to make me see stars, which was something that had never happened to me before.

I twisted my wrist, and flicked my fingers faster, feeling a rush of wetness from her folds when I did. I needed her to be as far gone as I was. I needed her to have the same unforgettable memory of this moment that I was undoubtedly going to have. Moving my mouth to the side of her neck, I kissed my way to her rapid pulse, and shifted my hand caught between her thighs so I could brush my knuckles against the tight, tiny bump of her clit. Her body jolted at the contact, and her hand tightened to where she was stroking me into an almost painful hold.

Her eyes flew open and her jaw dropped just slightly. "Do that again." Her teeth bit into her lip and she suddenly looked shy. "Please."

Vaguely, I recalled our previous conversation about dating. She mentioned she hadn't really seen anyone aside from that asshole Richard. It wasn't a stretch to imagine the selfish, annoying man as a terrible lover. She was probably too inexperienced and unpracticed to know what it was like when the man she was with put her desire and needs in front of his own.

"Whatever you want, I'll give it to you." Somewhere in the back of my mind, I wanted that declaration to carry its weight outside of the bedroom...but it couldn't. And I knew that. At least not right now.

I used my thumb to rub soft circles around her most sensitive of spots, increasing the pressure and speed until she was panting and writhing beneath me. I grunted in surprise when her teeth suddenly locked down on my shoulder as her back bowed off the bed. Her fingers flicked briefly along the heavy vein on the underneath side of my cock, and that pulse of pleasure low in my gut started to blaze outward. All of my nerves felt electrified, and my heart started to pound so hard and fast I wondered if she could hear it.

The sound of blood rushing was so loud I almost didn't hear her small shout of completion. But I sure felt it.

Her delicate frame shook so hard she almost dislodged my still-playing fingers. A rush of wetness suddenly surrounded my touch and made the glide of my fingers through her delicate folds even easier. Feeling her release, knowing I was the one who wrung all the pleasure from her body, was enough to send my own release spiraling out of control. A second later, her fingers were the ones coated in moisture.

It took a while before either of us moved. All things considered, this was hands down the best, most erotic, foreplay I'd ever been a part of. I wanted to strip her the rest of the way out of her dress, throw the remaining pieces of my suit on the floor, and fuck her until the sun came up. But, that thinking was dangerous, and I'd already crossed more than one invisible line I'd drawn for myself when I agreed to this scheme of hers.

Planting a hard, nearly bruising kiss on her soft mouth, I levered myself off of her now-pliant body and flopped face down on the mattress next to her. I needed to strip out of my damp underwear and get my racing heart and wavering sensibilities back under control.

"I like you far more than I ever anticipated, Langley Vaughn." And that was a problem.

She turned her head, and I had to close my eyes to block out the seductive gleam in hers. How someone could be so equally tempting and innocent was a mystery.

"I like you a lot as well, Iker Alvarez." She sounded far less surprised by the revelation than I did, and I wondered if she was still going to like me when the truth about why we could never have anything more than this week was revealed.

Part of me wanted to believe she would understand. But a bigger part reminded me we were worlds apart, and as kind and thoughtful as she was, she really didn't understand what it was like and what it meant to give up everything for someone else.

Chapter 9

Langley

What were the chances of falling for someone in six days?

It's just an infatuation, I reminded myself. A crush. Our emotions were heightened by the stress of the week, we'd been together every single day, and we had some off-the-charts chemistry. Add that all together, and there was bound to be an infatuation.

Right. I was infatuated with him.

Infatuated with his strength of heart, of character, how he stood up for me when even I honestly believed I couldn't.

Infatuated with the way he looked at me—like I was a puzzle to solve. Like I was something special and deserved to be treated as such.

Infatuated with the low timbre of his voice, and just about everything he said.

Infatuated with his dimple.

God, I loved that dimple, his smile, his laugh. I loved everything about his body, really. All cut and hard, with yards of tan skin stretching over stacked muscle. Loved the way he'd touched me last night, how he'd drawn reactions out of me I didn't know I had.

Iker stripped my inhibitions in just about every way possible, and I loved it—his effect on me.

Stop using that word. One orgasm does not the L-word make.

I sighed, thinking of how he'd kissed his way up my naked spine as he'd zipped this dress. The elevator *dinged* on the floor, jarring me from my Iker-induced haze, and I stepped onto the soft carpet.

My fingers barely rapped on the door once before it was thrown open.

"She's here!" Nessa cried out, then yanked me inside.

The Penrose suite was three bedrooms of over-the-top luxury, so naturally, Camille had chosen this one.

"You were supposed to be here four hours ago!" Virginia shouted, coming out of one of the bedrooms with both her finger and temper raised.

"Three and a half," I answered with a shrug. "And I'm here now. It's not like I missed the wedding, just all the veiled insults you would have thrown my way all afternoon. So, I really saved us both the effort."

Virginia's mouth dropped open, which I understood. Hell, I was kind of shocked I'd actually said it too.

"We only have a half hour until we have to leave for the chapel," she seethed.

"Oh, that's plenty of time for you to cut me down to size, no worries." I turned to where Phoebe and Nessa stood in their pink dresses, watching us like a tennis match. "You girls look lovely!" *Like cotton candy at a county fair*, I thought to myself.

"Your hair isn't done—" Virginia started.

"Oh, it's done, it's just not up." I'd washed, dried, and curled it a little.

"I can give it a simple twist," the hairdresser commented, sticking his head outside the bedroom.

"Sure, if that's what Camille would like, then I'm happy to do that." See, I could totally be accommodating.

"She asked that all the bridesmaids wear their hair up," Virginia hissed, following me into the bedroom with the stylist.

"Oh, I'm sorry," I told her as I sat on the pretty, cushioned stool beside the vanity. "When was this announcement?"

"She decided this afternoon." Virginia's reflection hovered behind me in the mirror.

"Huh," I said, checking my phone. "I guess I missed that text."

The stylist hid a laugh as he started to comb my hair.

"You would have known if you'd been here."

"I figured if it was that important that I witness the worship of Camille, you would have sent someone to fetch me to kneel at the altar of her ego. But since there was no knock, and no text, and zero apology from anyone about what happened last night, I got ready in my own room, and had a lovely day of it." I smiled especially bright, which sent splotches of red up her neck.

Just as her mouth opened to retort, a shrill cry sounded from the other room.

"Mom! My tiara is all wrong!"

Virginia shook her head at me, then fled this bedroom in favor of the one that no doubt held Camille. "I'm coming, Cammy!"

"Hi. I'm Langley," I told the stylist as his nimble fingers worked my hair into a classic French twist.

"Hi, Langley, I'm Daniel, and I've heard all sorts of *interesting* things about you today." He gave me a wink.

"Remind me to give you a huge tip. I'm sure you'll need it to hit the bar after being in here all afternoon with these vipers."

He laughed, but didn't disagree, and twenty minutes later, I was styled and ready to walk out with the bridal party.

"So, you do live," Camille snapped at me as Virginia fluffed what looked to be about fourteen layers of tulle on her.

"And you look beautiful," I told her honestly. Was the dress a little much? Maybe, but so was Camille. The dress was as over-the-top as everything else about this wedding was.

Her eyes narrowed, but there was zero malice in my comment to strike back on. It was her day, even if she was a witch.

We made our way down to the lobby, pink peonies in hand, just like Camille had wanted. I smiled when instructed by the photographer, and squeezed into the limo with the other girls. Stuffing Camille and her dress in took a little time, and was definitely not one of the things she wanted photographed.

The drive to the chapel was four minutes, at most—just around the little lake, but the walk would have been killer in that dress and the heels.

"Okay, just as planned, everyone," the coordinator told us after speaking into her headset.

We sat through the production of unfolding Camille from the car, and then straightened our knee-length dresses after we climbed out.

The June air hung heavy, fragrant with the flowers that had been draped along the railings of the steps leading into the chapel. It was perfect, really.

"What?" I heard the coordinator whisper into her headset. "You're certain?"

Every head pivoted toward her. She faked a smile at Camille and held up her finger. "Well, you should do that *right now*," she spoke into the headset.

"What's wrong?" Camille asked, voice shrill and high.

"Well, we've arrived before the groom, so—"

"What?" Camille shouted. "He's not here?"

"I'm sure he's on his way, so we need to get you inside, so he doesn't see you before the wedding." The coordinator's smile shook.

"It's okay, baby. Let's just get you inside. Pamela, find him!" Virginia ordered the coordinator with a pointed stare.

Pamela might need a big tip too, even though she was already getting paid a small fortune.

We shuffled inside, quickly shutting the door to the bridal room so Richard wouldn't see Camille when he walked into the chapel.

That is, if *he walked into the chapel.*

Looking at the red-hot anger in her eyes, I wasn't sure he'd want to see her first, anyway.

Virginia consoled Camille in the corner as Nessa and I stood by the door.

"Think he jilted her?" she whispered.

"I'd like to say no, but I honestly have no clue what Richard might do anymore," I answered. I wished I'd had my phone so I could text Iker, but Camille had banned them in the bridal party, just in case one of us got trigger happy on an Instagram photo before she could release the professionally edited ones.

"Okay, he's twenty minutes out," Pamela said with a look of relief on her face. Obviously, she'd wondered if Camille was going to be jilted too.

"The hotel is like…three minutes away. How the hell can he be so far away?" Camille snapped.

"I believe there was an error in judgment about what time the men needed to begin getting ready," Pamela answered.

"AKA, Richard is hungover," Nessa replied in a whisper.

"Or already drunk again," Phoebe agreed.

Virginia left the room to go find my father, and I slowly crossed the floor to where Camille was pacing, fisting her hands in the fluffy tulle of her dress.

"Stop," I told her. "You're wrinkling the material."

Surprisingly, she did as I commanded.

Her chest shook as she sucked in a breath, and I smoothed out the skirt where she'd rumpled it.

"Okay, that's better," I said softly, making sure her tiara and veil were still straight.

"You must be loving this." There was a sadness in her tone I'd never heard before, and more than a touch of fear that I picked up on.

"Of course not," I told her. "I have never wanted you to be unhappy Camille. Ever."

She blinked back tears. "I can't believe he did this."

"Me either. But Richard is..." I shook my head, looking for the right words.

"Selfish? Conceited?" she suggested.

I laughed. "Yes, all that." *And then some.*

"I love him, though, in spite of...everything. We're perfectly matched. We understand each other." She glanced up at the clock. "The wedding was supposed to start fifteen minutes ago."

"It can't start without you. And I'm glad you love him. It would be a shame to spend the rest of your life with the wrong person just to prove a point." The door opened and Virginia hurried inside, my dad in tow. "Be happy, Camille. Because I'm going to be."

With those words, I retreated, leaving Virginia to fuss over Camille.

"He's here!" The relief practically exploded from Pamela's voice.

There was a flurry of activity, and then we all headed for the door as Pamela stage-whispered orders.

"You look beautiful, Langley," Dad told me, kissing my cheek as the music started up.

"You look great in a tux, Dad."

He laughed, but ran his hands down the lapels. "I was talking with Iker out there. You know he could have worn his dress blues instead of a tux."

"I just wanted him to be comfortable."

"Trust me, soldiers are way more comfortable in uniform, even dress mess, than we are in these monkey suits."

That brought a smile to my face. "We, huh?"

He shrugged boyishly. "He kind of reminds me of me when I was that age. What?" he said as I gaped at him. "He honestly does. The military is a great equalizer. Enlisted guys all start at the same level and work their way up on their own merit. It was the one time in my life it didn't matter that I came from money."

"Or that Iker doesn't?"

"Exactly. He's making rank fast, especially for his age. That says way more about his character than any trust fund could. You know, I was kind of worried the guy would run for the hills after last night, but he must be crazy about you, because he's still here."

I swallowed the tiny knot of deceit that tangled my vocal cords. He was here because I paid him to be. But was that really the only reason? I couldn't be the only one feeling that this was more than just a transaction, not with the way he'd put his hands on me last night. It hadn't been just sexual. At least, I knew it hadn't only been sexual for me.

"He's a really good guy," I managed to get out.

Dad looked back to Camille, who stood with Virginia, their heads bent close in a conversation we couldn't hear. She'd asked both Dad and Virginia to walk her down the aisle.

"She really does look beautiful, doesn't she?" I asked, nodding toward Camille.

My father's eyes softened, the expression lines deepening as he smiled. "She does. I do love her, though I'm starting to see that maybe I've been a little blind to the fact that she hasn't loved *you*. There are going to have to be some changes."

I blinked back my own tears as the music swelled. It was nearly my turn. "It's okay," I assured him. "I'm happy as long as you're happy." I motioned to the door. "I think I'm on deck."

Pamela nodded, waving me closer.

"I'm glad you're here for her," I told Dad. "Glad that she has you."

"Of course," he replied with a serious nod. "After all, I had to practice so I can be perfect when the guy who's actually worthy of *you* stands at the end of that aisle. This is just my trial run for the real thing one day."

I squeezed his hand, my words failing as tears threatened to form, and then I walked that perfect, peony-decked aisle, my eyes finding Iker, and staying there.

He'd turned in his pew to watch me, his lips turned up, but no dimple.

I nearly stumbled as I came closer to him. He was heart-stoppingly, panty-meltingly gorgeous, and even in a room full of elegant men in designer tuxedos, he stood out, because unlike other men, Iker made the tux look good, not the other way around.

We broke eye contact as I passed, and I took my place on the tiered steps.

Camille made her entrance, and the first time I even looked at Richard was when I took Camille's bouquet so she could join hands with him. Richard's expression was the perfect combination of chagrined and awestruck, topped with a hint of hungover. He was clearly regretting his drunken outburst last night, and slightly overwhelmed by the events happening today. He really was a man-child, and I was glad I wasn't the one stuck waiting for him to grow the hell up.

My eyes strayed to Iker all through the ceremony.

His were always on me.

We were separated by at least twenty feet, but his gaze made my skin ache for his touch with the same intensity as when we'd been separated by only a few layers of fabric.

Tonight was our last night, according to our bargain, but I wanted—I needed—more. I needed him in my life with his laser-tag nobility and fearlessness. Needed his smile, his kiss, the way he made me feel like I could fly if I just spread my wings and launched.

But what did I bring to the table for him? He didn't care about my money, my status, or my manners, which had been touted as my three finest features for the last five years. I had a crazy family that came with a rigid set of rules, and Iker had nothing but disdain for my world. Why the hell would he even want to stick around?

But then he grinned, that dimple popping into his cheek, and I didn't care about any of it.

Not the expectations, or the rules. Not the differences in our worlds, or the many ways he was way too good for a pain in the ass like me.

I cared about two things: I wanted him and he wanted me.

Everything else could work itself out.

"I now pronounce you man and wife," the preacher said, and then we were clapping.

Richard and Camille kissed, and then we followed them down the aisle, the entourage that hadn't changed since high school.

Well, *they* hadn't changed.

I was beginning to think that maybe I had.

The newlyweds disappeared into the bridal room, and bottles of bubbles were thrust into our hands as we were ushered out to wait on the steps.

Complete with a peony-laden carriage.

As Iker walked toward me, my vision of the perfect wedding changed. I didn't need the Broadmoor, or the carriage. Maybe just a beach, a few friends, and family. Maybe Vegas with a singing Elvis. Maybe a tiny town in the mountains. Definitely not this kind of spectacle.

Camille could have her fireworks display as long as I had fireworks in my marriage—whenever I decided to marry, that is.

Iker's hands wrapped around my waist, and he pulled me against his chest with a soft kiss.

"What were you grinning about?" I asked him, running my thumb over his dimple.

"I was wondering what you were smiling about the whole time," he answered.

"Me?"

"Yeah, you were pretty much ear to ear." He kissed me again, and I let myself melt into him for those seconds our mouths lingered.

I heard the snap of a camera and saw the photographer walking away as Iker and I broke apart, but kept our fingers intertwined for the few moments we had before it was time to blow bubbles for Camille and Richard.

They climbed into the carriage and drove away, two matching, white horses pulling them back toward the hotel.

"You did great up there," Iker told me. "I knew you wouldn't break down, but I was afraid of how deep the whole thing could cut you."

"I wasn't really paying attention," I admitted. Surprisingly enough, it was the truth. My thoughts hadn't been on the loss of the life I could have had, but the potential of the life I could actually have if I was just brave enough to say the words and ask him if he felt the same.

"I noticed."

We stood there for a second, looking at each other, oblivious to the movement of the crowd around us.

"Langley!" Nessa called out to me from the limo.

"I have to go take pictures."

"I'll meet you over at the reception," he promised as he walked me to the waiting car.

As the rest of the bridal party piled in, I rose on my toes and pressed a kiss to Iker's cheek, then let my lips linger at his ear. "Want to know what I'll be thinking until then?"

"Yes." His hands held my hips, his fingers warm enough to feel through the silk of my dress.

"How to get your hands on me later." I let my teeth graze his earlobe, and was rewarded with a squeeze of his hands.

Then it was his lips at the shell of my ear, sending shivers down my spine. "I'll be thinking about how to keep my hands *off* you at the reception." He pressed a hot kiss to the spot just under my ear, and I was ready to skip the reception. Cake was overrated.

"Langley!" Nessa shouted from the door of the limo.

"You should think less," I teased him, sliding out of his arms.

"Pictures. Go. Now. Before I send those hands you're thinking about up your smooth thighs." His playful tone was at odds with the intensity in his eyes.

"Promises, promises," I told him, bending to slide into the limo next to Nessa, flashing him a little peek of the thighs he'd just mentioned.

He shook his head at me with a grin, and shut the door.

I smiled all through the pictures, especially the ones where I got to cuddle next to Iker and piss Camille off at the same time. She grumbled about his visible tattoos more than once, but we both pretended not to hear a thing. I was too busy thinking of all the ways I was going to make sure this wasn't my last night with Iker.

I wanted as many nights as he had to give me.

Chapter 10

Iker

"It's been a long time since I've seen Langley smile that way."

I shot a surprised glance at Langley's father when he sat down in the vacant seat next to mine. He had a crystal glass with a shot of something I would guess was whiskey or bourbon in his hand, but his eyes were on his daughter who was doing the obligatory chicken dance. I flat-out refused, but promised her I would get up and shake it for the next song.

Picking up my beer, I told him, "She's a tough cookie. Much stronger than I thought she would be when we first met. She's also very selfless. She puts everyone else's wants and needs before her own without complaint. She should have some fun and get to smile like that more often."

The older man swirled the amber liquid in his glass and I heard him sigh. "She's been taking care of me for a very long time. When her mother got sick, I sort of lost my purpose and drive. Langley kept our entire lives on track when she was just a child. One of the reasons I initially fell for Virginia was because she was so devoted to Camille. Her entire world revolves around her daughter and I foolishly believed that devotion would carry over to Langley once we got married. It wasn't until this wedding, and everything with that prick Richard came about, that my eyes were really opened to the fact that Langley is hardly more than a second thought to my wife...or her own daughter."

I snorted, which drew his attention fully toward me. "Your wife treats Langley like garbage. She speaks to her as if she's an intruder in your home. She's totally unsympathetic to any little part of her mother Langley has tried to hold onto, and she does nothing to dissuade the unwarranted feud between the girls. In fact, I think she encourages it. From the outside looking in, it's almost as if your new wife is afraid you don't have enough love to go around, so she wants to make sure she and her daughter get the bulk of it. She's fine with Langley getting scraps."

The man stiffened next to me, and his drink hit the table with a *thud*. I had nothing to lose and someone needed to tell the man the truth about the things happening in his own home. "You didn't just throw Langley to the wolves, you moved them into her home and expected her to figure out how to fight them on her own."

Corbin Vaughn cleared his throat and leaned back in his chair. "If things have been that bad at home, why didn't she ever tell me?"

I lifted a shoulder and let it fall carelessly. "Because she loves you. Because, for whatever reason, you're happy with that harpy you married. Because she knows, eventually, she will be living on her own, making her own choices, and far out of the reach of both her stepmother and stepsister. Mostly, she's a good girl, one who loves her father unconditionally, so she's done what she's had to do, and endured every moment to keep the peace."

The older man sighed again and reached for his drink. "I never intended to put so much on her, especially with this wedding. I should have put my foot down when Camille demanded she be in the wedding party. I knew it was going to be hard for Langley, but I caved. I told her things were going to have to change. I need to be more accountable if I don't want to lose my daughter when she does have her own life to focus on."

I reached out and tapped the tip of my beer bottle with his abandoned glass. "Sounds like a plan."

He chuckled and I felt his hand land on my shoulder with a thump. "How is it you've known my daughter for such a short while and recognized she was suffering silently, and I've been blind to it all these years?"

I shrugged again. "She doesn't have to put on an act with me. There's nothing to lose when she's real with me. If she does that with you, she has to admit to how hard things have been for her when all she wants is for you to believe things are fine. She has to tell you the truth that your happiness is ultimately the reason she's miserable." He had to know she was too selfless to ever do that.

At least one of us was totally honest when we were together. I hadn't exactly lied to Langley, but there were definitely things I had omitted, things that more than likely would've kept us from getting as close as we had so quickly.

Langley's father released his hold on my shoulder as the woman we were talking about suddenly turned and started to make her way in our direction. Somehow, she managed to make the poufy, pink dress look good. She still resembled a piece of candy, but I had no problem imagining how sweet she would taste underneath the clingy fabric.

"I'm happy she found someone whom she could share how she was feeling with. I'm glad you've been there for her this last week. I wouldn't mind seeing more of you around the house, Iker. I know you both mentioned your relationship is casual, but my daughter looks at you like you hung the moon. That isn't the definition of casual in my book."

It was the perfect opportunity to tell him I wasn't going to be around the house, or anywhere else for that matter, after tonight. He was former military, he would understand, but I couldn't force the words out. Couldn't tell him the truth when I hadn't been totally honest with Langley. Even if he would be more sympathetic to my predicament.

The moment was lost when the woman I couldn't stop thinking about appeared at her father's side. He rose when Langley reached the table, bending down so he could brush a light kiss on her flushed cheek.

"I'm so glad this wedding is almost over." He muttered the words quietly under his breath, but they were loud enough to pull a laugh from Langley and a chuckle from me.

He abandoned his now-empty drink and made his way in the direction of his wife. Langley's stepmother was standing by the bar, a sour look on her face. I had a pang of regret that I wouldn't be around when the horrid woman was finally knocked down a peg or two.

My phone buzzed, and I swiped it open, my stomach sinking at the platoon-wide thread. Nothing like a small change to the schedule to get everyone in an uproar, including me. I wanted every single second I had left with Langley. I quickly typed my acknowledgement of the change, hit enter, and put my phone away as Langley sat.

"What were you and my dad talking about so seriously over here?" Her hand landed on the top of my thigh, which immediately made my dick twitch.

"About how pretty you looked today, and about what a trooper you are for getting through this wedding with a smile." I put my hand over the top of hers and gave it a little squeeze. "It's almost over."

Neither of us missed the double meaning behind that statement. All of it was almost over. The reality of the situation felt like a lead stone in my gut and had bitter regret rising in the back of my throat.

"Are you sure you weren't making fun of me doing the chicken dance?" Her gold-tinted eyebrows danced upward, and her teeth flashed as she smiled at me.

I shifted closer to her so I could touch my lips to the soft curve of her cheek. "Cutest pink chicken ever."

She laughed, tossing her head back and looking more carefree and relaxed than she had since we'd met.

"Come on." She tugged on my hand until I got to my feet. "You promised to dance with me."

I followed willingly. I could hold my own on a dance floor, and I wasn't about to pass up the opportunity to hold Langley close while she wiggled and shook her booty all up on me. Plus, there was bound to be a slow dance or two somewhere in the mix. I was very much looking forward to swaying with her in the dark, holding onto her like she belonged to me. It almost felt like if I pretended hard enough, I could make keeping her a reality.

"You're a good dancer." Her hands slid across my shoulders and pulled me closer.

I arched an eyebrow and gave her a smirk. "Why do you sound surprised? Just because I didn't know how to foxtrot or waltz doesn't mean I don't know how to dance."

She gave a graceful shrug and giggled when I spun her around in a twirl. "I guess my image of the big, strong soldier didn't include good rhythm and fancy footwork."

The smirk turned into a wicked leer. "If you want to test out just how good my rhythm is, I am more than happy to oblige you, sweetheart."

A mischievous twinkle lit up her blue eyes and my body instantly reacted. This girl affected me in ways no other had. She'd fallen into my life exactly when I needed her, but the timing couldn't be worse. The irony of that was incredible.

Shaking my head to dislodge the dark, negative thoughts trying to pull my attention away from the pretty princess in my arms, I forced a grin and lowered my head so I could whisper in her ear, "How soon can we dip out of here? I've been thinking about getting you alone since you crawled out of bed this morning." I really needed to sit her down and explain things to her. I couldn't leave her in the dark. No doubt she would find a way to blame herself if I left without a trace. "I want to talk to you about something."

I small furrow tugged at her blonde brows and her pert little nose wrinkled. "Is this about the rest of the money I owe you? I have it upstairs in my bag. I meant to give it you last night after the rehearsal, but...I got distracted."

She blushed, and I chuckled when thinking about exactly how I'd kept her distracted after her ex's drunken nonsense the night before.

"I know you're good for the money. I'm not worried about it." I couldn't believe the words coming out of my mouth. It would be so much easier to simply remind her the only reason I was here with her tonight was because she was paying me. But, I couldn't belittle her, or the way she made me feel by hiding behind that lie anymore. I was here because she was here. There was nothing more to it. "I want to talk to you about something else."

The hope that brightened her eyes was like a dagger through my heart. I should've been honest with her from the start. As soon as I realized she wasn't an entitled, stuck-up snob, I should've come clean. I knew from the start we were playing a game, but I never anticipated hearts getting involved. That made the situation so much more complicated and convoluted.

Exhaling a long, slow breath, I pulled Langley to my chest as the beat switched to a slow, romantic ballad. She tucked her head under my chin and her arms wrapped around my waist. Once again, I was baffled by how well we fit together. She was not a girl made for me, so there was no reason for her to fill my arms—and the empty spot in my heart—like she was custom-made to belong there.

Langley sighed and bent her head so that her forehead was resting against the hollow of my throat. I'd ditched the bowtie hours ago so I could feel her warm skin against mine. Her arms tightened around my waist as if she was trying to hold onto something she knew was fleeting.

"Let's save any serious conversation for tomorrow. We made it through the wedding. Everyone is unscathed. Camille is going on her honeymoon, so the house will be quiet until she gets back. Richard showed his true colors. Right now, I want to focus on dancing with the hottest guy in the room...and whatever comes next. The real world can wait. Going back to your regular responsibilities can wait. Just give me tonight." Her tone held a hint of sadness, almost as if she knew tonight was really all I could give her.

Blowing out another deep breath, I dropped a kiss on her forehead and ran my palm up her back until I was cupping the back of her neck. "All right. Tonight is yours. I'm yours to do with as you please."

I felt her smile against my throat. "That's a dangerous declaration but one I'm more than willing to oblige."

I chuckled and tugged her even closer. We were hardly dancing any longer, more just our bodies swaying to the slow song while we held onto one another.

"Pretty sure whatever you ask me for, I'm more than willing to give you. You deserve everything, Langley. Don't settle for less." She needed to find someone who reminded her that her happiness was just as important as everyone else's in her life. She should find someone who made that killer smile of hers a permanent expression on her flawless face.

Even if I could stick around, I wasn't sure that guy was me. I'd seen too much, lived too hard, spread myself too thin on the regular to be the type of guy wholly dedicated to making a good girl like Langley's life easier. Sure, being together right now was fun and fairly easy, but when the actuality of the people we were in the real world hit, nothing about the two of us trying to make a relationship work would be smooth sailing. All those differences which we found intriguing and interesting now would become nothing but burdensome in the long run.

Suddenly, she tilted her head back, and I swore it would be so effortless to drown in the ocean blue of her eyes. I was already weak where she was concerned and not at all a very good swimmer.

"Right now, I think I deserve a drink. After that, I want to take these heels off and see how long it takes me to peel you out of that tux. In the morning, I'll remember none of this is real and we need to talk, but tonight...let's pretend." Her voice had a sing-song quality to it that was deceptively cheerful. It was a good reminder she was quicker than people gave her credit for and a master at reading people's emotions behind the façade they tended to wear. I was no exception. She always managed to see more than I intended to show her.

I cupped her face in my hands and placed a slow, tender kiss on her lips. I might not get to kiss her goodbye once she knew everything, but there was no way I could leave her without stealing one.

"A drink and a night of make-believe it is. Tell me all your dreams, and I'll make them come true." I flashed her a playful wink and followed her laugher off the crowded dance floor.

That clock ticking down in the back of my head was getting louder and louder. And the ache in my chest was getting more and more painful by the second.

I tried to ignore both. I was determined to give Langley a night she would never forget. I wanted to be a memory she eventually looked back on fondly, instead of one filled with longing and regret.

And if I was being honest with myself, which would be a first this week, I wanted to make sure no matter how hard she tried, she couldn't forget me.

Chapter 11

Langley

Iker touched me the whole way back to our suite. Light caresses on my waist in the elevator, holding hands as we walked down the hallway, and fingers trailing my spine as we approached our door had my nerves firing on every possible level.

My skin felt aware, hyper-sensitive, and I was more than ready to get this dress off.

"What's that?" Iker asked as I dropped my clutch on the table at the entryway, his voice nearly drowned out by a loud *boom*.

His head snapped toward the window, his eyes narrowed and alert. Then he opened the French doors that led to our balcony. "Damn. She actually has fireworks."

I followed him out, leaning next to him against the balcony as we stared up at the colorful explosions that cost enough to put Iker's brother through another couple years of school. "I'm sorry; I should have warned you. They're ridiculous, but beautiful."

"You're beautiful."

Startled, I found him watching me. He brushed a strand of fallen hair back behind my ear.

Was he saying that because he meant it? Or because he was trying to give me my perfect night?

I mumbled my thank you and turned back to the display.

"You know that, right?" Iker asked, turning me so I faced him. The fireworks reflected in his dark eyes. He cupped my cheeks, then ran his hands along my jaw so his fingers laced at the base of my skull.

"Sure," I answered. "I happen to think you're way better-looking, but I'll let it slide."

The fake smile didn't fool him, and he leaned so his forehead rested against mine. "Not just the outside, though, that's pretty fucking spectacular too. You're beautiful here." He placed one hand over my heart, where skin met the neckline of my dress.

Could he feel my heart pounding?

"The loyalty you have to your dad, the way you can stand beside your stepsister while she's marrying your ex—"

"You don't think that makes me weak? Spineless?" I whispered my own fears, his lips only a breath away.

"I think it takes a metric-shit-ton of class to do what you've pulled off this week."

"I couldn't have done it without you." I closed the inches between us, kissing him slowly, moving my lips on his the way I'd wanted to all night.

His tongue licked along the seam of my lips, and I parted for him, sighing as his tongue rubbed against mine.

He tasted like those peppermints he so obviously loved and something dark and spicy, something uniquely Iker.

My arms wound around his neck, and I rose on my toes, our height difference even more noticeable without my shoes. I wanted to get closer, until there was nothing between us—not our clothes, our lifestyles, or our upbringings.

His hands drifted to my ass, and his groan rumbled against my breasts, tightening my nipples as he lifted me. My legs wrapped around his waist, my ankles locking at the small of his back as I deepened our kiss.

He switched the angle, and our kiss changed from slow to urgent, from soft to primal. My thighs clenched as that sweet hum of need in my belly caught fire. Maybe I'd curse myself in the morning because taking this transaction to the next level meant almost certain heartbreak, but I'd deal with that tomorrow.

Tonight was for losing myself in Iker.

As if the universe heard my thoughts, the fireworks came to a climax, then ceased.

"They're over," I said against his lips, my breath ragged.

"Only out there," he answered, and then carried me into the suite like I weighed next to nothing. The man was stacked with muscles I couldn't wait to trace with my tongue. Last night had been good—so good—but I hadn't explored him nearly enough.

His tongue was in my mouth, my fingers gripping his hair as we entered the bedroom.

Then he pulled away, and set me on my feet when I tried to bring his lips back to mine.

"Langley," he said, his tone even, voice steady.

"Hmmm?" I asked, my fingers deftly untying his bowtie and pulling it free.

"Langley," he repeated, more urgent, his hands holding my shoulders as he stepped back, putting all that cold space between us.

"Yes?" My lips tingled, my breasts felt heavy, and my pulse raced. How the hell was he so calm? So collected?

"I need you to think about this," he said slowly, enunciating each word carefully.

"Okay." I tilted my head. "Thought about it." Had been, thinking about it since that first impulsive kiss.

His elbows stayed locked, keeping me right where I was.

"I'm serious. I need to know that you'll be okay with this in the morning." His eyes glittered with an intensity I hadn't seen from him before, and since I'd watched him take down those two punks in the parking lot that night and Richard down yesterday, that was saying something.

"I'll be more than okay with it," I assured him. "Want me to sign something? Swear on a Bible? I'll even put my selfie on your Instagram with a caption that says *I'm about to have sex with this girl.*" That would be pretty fitting, considering how he'd gotten me to go have coffee with him that first night.

"God, no," he blurted.

My eyes dropped from his...landing on my open and messy suitcase where the envelope waited with the other five thousand I owed him. Because I paid him to be here. Had asked him to stand by me this week, and he had. Asked him to give me the perfect night...and he was.

"Oh shit, you don't want me." My mouth ran away from my brain, spewing thoughts I normally would have kept censored because that was what was expected of me. "I pressured you into this. I'm so sorry."

"What? Langley, no." Those hands that had been holding me back now gripped, keeping me from fleeing. "Look at me."

I brought my eyes to his slowly, taking in the strong line of his jaw, the full lips I couldn't seem to stop kissing, and finally reaching those dark depths that saw way too much. "I'm looking."

He took my hand and cupped it around his dick. His very hard, very ready dick.

"Does that feel like I don't want you?" He closed his eyes and mumbled, "I swear, this can only happen to me when I try to do the honorable thing..."

I squeezed gently and his breath left in a hiss. That reaction, the power I had in that moment, was heady.

"I've wanted you since the moment I saw you in that bar, all wide eyes and curves. I taste you in my sleep, and wake up desperate to see you, to touch you. Fuck, even the sound of your voice turns me on. And you think I don't want you?" His eyes narrowed. "All I want is you in that bed, naked, under me, screaming out my name while I find out all the different ways I can make you come."

His words sent a shot of heat to my core so strong that I nearly swayed.

"Yes, please."

"There's no taking this back."

"I won't ever want to," I promised him. I abandoned his erection to unbutton his shirt, slipping the little disks free, one by one, as he stared at me.

I kissed each inch of bared skin, until I tugged the shirt free from his pants. His skin was golden, smooth and soft, completely opposite to the hard lines of his abs. His breathing picked up as my fingers reached to trace the lines of the tattoo on his side.

Then he muttered a curse, ripping out his cufflinks, which fell to the floor with any second thoughts I might have.

A second later, his shirt and jacket were gone and I was pressed up against all that warm skin as he kissed me senseless.

He didn't stop kissing me while we undressed, simply moved his mouth to my neck, my collarbone, the extra sensitive back of my neck as he unzipped my dress. Once it was puddled around my ankles, I stepped free, leaving me in nothing but my blush-colored strapless bra and matching thong.

His eyes swept over me hungrily as he stripped down to his boxer-briefs, which were stretched with the strain of containing him.

He took a condom from his wallet and tossed it onto the nightstand, raising his eyebrows in question.

Did I know where this was leading? Hell yes, I did.

I stepped forward the same moment he did, and we met in a clash of tongue and teeth. His fingers pulled the pins from my hair until it fell against my back in a heavy wave.

Then, silky softness was at my back and Iker was above me, kissing me with an expertise I knew had already ruined the chances of any guy who might come after him.

He was hard between my thighs, rocking against me, sending off a set of my own fireworks through my abdomen each time he brushed against me.

"Beautiful," he said after he sent my bra to meet my dress, and my back bowed as he sucked my nipple between his lips.

This man turned me into liquid fire.

His hands stroked my waist as he worshiped his way down my body. He took his time, lingering on the spots that made me gasp, sucking a small raspberry into the hollow right above my hip bone... like he'd wanted to mark me in only a place that only the two of us would ever know each time I touched that spot.

His eyes locked with mine as he slid my underwear down my thighs, my calves, my feet, until I was bare before him. It was quite possibly the most erotic moment I'd ever experienced.

"Damn, Langley," he said with equal parts reverence and lust as he looked at my naked body.

Confidence had never been my strong suit, but his gaze didn't just make me feel sexy, it made me feel like I was his equal. That we were on a level playing field when it came to how badly we wanted each other.

Then my thoughts stopped as he parted my thighs, then my cleft, and set his mouth on me.

"Iker!" My hips bucked against his face, and he slipped my thighs over his arms and settled in like he had no other plans for the evening.

My hands clenched the covers as he ripped away every thought with his nimble tongue. I couldn't think, couldn't speak, could only feel. His teeth were sharp as they grazed my clit, his tongue soft as it stroked, then firm as it darted inside me.

He didn't back down, didn't tease, and didn't grow bored or impatient. He built my pleasure like an architect, and when all that tension coiled in my belly, my muscles locking, he pushed me right over the edge and then held me there as my orgasm hit wave after wave.

I fell limp against the bed as it receded, my mind and body equally blissed out.

Iker rose above me, pausing to lose his boxer-briefs.

"That was... You're. Wow." One look at his hard, lean body, and the desire I thought was satisfied flared back to life when he grinned, that damn, irresistible dimple making an appearance.

"We're just getting started," he promised as he sheathed himself. Something shifted in his eyes, a longing I couldn't quite identify before he bent his head to kiss his way up my neck. "I never want to leave this bed."

I'd only ever been with Richard, and he never made me feel this desirable, this necessary.

Everything with Iker felt new, and so erotic, and I wanted this feeling to last forever.

"I'm okay with that."

His mouth met mine as he lowered his hips between my thighs. The kiss was as messy as my feelings for him, and I threw myself into it, savoring every second I could get with him.

He rocked against me, the head of his erection nudging my entrance, and I moaned.

"Tell me you want this," he said, his voice strained, his eyes locked on mine.

"I want you."

"God help me, you're *all* I want," he swore, then pushed inside me in one smooth, long thrust that kept going and going.

I rippled around him, my back arching as sensation took over. He filled me completely, then stretched my body, claiming every inch and demanding more until he was seated to the hilt, his forehead on mine and our breathing equally ragged as he slowed his pace.

"You're huge," I managed in between breaths as I adjusted and eased around him.

"You sure know how to make a guy feel good about himself," he replied, his smile tight. "You okay?"

My heart slipped. Even in this moment, when he was buried inside me, sweat beading his skin from the effort it took to maintain control, he put me first.

Stupid, foolish heart.

"More than okay." I drew my knees up and he slid impossibly deeper.

"Langley," he groaned. "God, you feel..." He tapered off as he withdrew almost to the tip, then thrust in again.

"Feel what?" I asked as pleasure washed over me.

"Good. Too good. Like something I'm not supposed to have."

I brushed my fingers along his jaw, which was already prickly. Then I slid my hands down his back to grip his ass.

"You already have me." The emotional impact of the words hit me as his body began to move within mine. He did have me, and with each stroke, he took a little more.

I had no idea who I'd be in the morning, but I couldn't wait to meet her.

The rhythm was slow, his thrusts deep and powerful. I met him at every turn, our bodies joining like we'd been making love for years, not minutes. When I started to whimper, losing myself to the incredible fire he built within me, he increased the pace.

Tension drew me taut as he thrust harder, faster.

"Iker," I pled, held on the precipice, dancing on the razor's edge of a pleasure so sharp I was almost scared to let go.

He brought my knee higher, switched his angle so he hit my clit every time he bottomed out within me, and kissed me deep.

The wire holding me to the Earth snapped, and I came, pleasure radiating through me deeper, harder than ever before, as I cried out into his mouth. There were no stars behind my eyes, just Iker above me, his thrusts uncontrolled, his breath ragged, his throat working as he broke our kiss.

Then it was my name on his lips as he shuddered deep within me, stilling above me in a moment of beautiful abandon before collapsing, his face buried in my neck.

He rolled to his side, bringing me with him so we faced each other.

My hand skimmed down his back, reveling in the ability to touch him, to feel him against me—inside me—like this.

I didn't want this to end. Any of it. I wanted to see him again tomorrow, and the next day, and the next.

I wanted us to be real.

I didn't want an envelope of cash being what kept him here longer.

Oh yeah, my heart was trying to jump ship.

"You okay?" I asked, turning his words back on him.

"More than okay," he answered with a soft kiss.

He excused himself to clean up, then tucked us both under the covers. His smile was sleepy, unguarded. I doubted many people got to see him like this, completely and utterly relaxed.

I had to tell him. Had to try. If I didn't, then I'd never know if we could be more, when it felt like we already were.

I could handle a no. At least, I was pretty sure I could. But I knew for certain I couldn't handle the what-if of us.

"Iker?"

"Langley?" His eyes lost the sleepy haze.

My fingers traced the roses on his side. "Um. So, no pressure, and this is probably the completely wrong time to ask, but I was wondering if maybe you wanted to go out next weekend?"

Asking a guy out while he was lying naked next to me was definitely a first.

The skin between his eyebrows puckered, and he gave me a look I couldn't translate. Longing? Regret? Need? Want? Somehow, they seemed to come in flashes and I couldn't grasp onto any one of them to fixate on.

"No pressure," I whispered, but even I heard the little break in my voice.

He tangled his hand in my hair, and then brought his lips to mine in a sipping kiss.

"Next weekend?" His lips moved to my jaw.

"Or the one after. I know you have a life that doesn't include society weddings every weekend." My breath caught as he started on my neck. How the hell could he turn me on when I'd already had two orgasms?

He gripped my waist, and rolled to his back, lifting me to straddle him.

"Why wait that long?" he asked as his thumbs found my nipples.

"Oh. You want sooner?" My thoughts scattered with each touch, and blew completely away when I felt him harden beneath me.

"Yeah, I was thinking right now."

He pulled me into his kiss and I agreed that next weekend was far too far away.

Now was definitely good.

Chapter 12

Iker

I woke up before the sun came up.

It was habit. Being in the army for as long as I'd been meant lazy mornings in bed were a rare occurrence. Part of me wanted nothing more than to snuggle into the luxurious bedding and sink into the sexy warmth of the soft body wrapped around mine, but a larger, louder part of me was screaming at me to move. To get up. To walk away. To minimize the damage done to this beautiful, brilliant girl as much as I could.

If only she hadn't asked to make plans in the future.

If only she hadn't responded so sweetly, so uninhibited to my every touch.

If only she wasn't the type of girl to promise to wait for me, to put her entire life on hold even though there was no guarantee I would make it back in one piece.

Sighing and feeling nearly suffocated by regret and remorse, I turned so I could lightly kiss Langley's forehead, biting back a grin as her eyebrows danced upward in her sleep. She looked like a thoroughly debauched angel, her halo lost somewhere on the floor with the rest of her clothes. It was a nice image to remember her by.

I inched my way out of the bed, careful to shift slow and steady when I dislodged her head from my arm. I planned to tell her face-to-face I was leaving...not just the state, but the country. I'd been silently counting down the days to my next deployment since before that fateful meeting with Langley in the bar that night.

I was only planning on sticking by her for a week, so initially, I didn't think it mattered if she knew I was getting ready to go wheels up or not. My real life didn't have anything to do with this somewhat dark fairytale she dragged me into... At least, not at first. Now, it felt like I'd deceived her, lied by omission. I allowed her to get attached, to get so much closer than I normally let anyone get, but I was still leaving and there was not a damn thing that could be done about it.

I pulled on my discarded pants from the night before and dragged my hands over my face. I couldn't help shooting another look over my shoulder at the woman sleeping behind me. My fingers itched to reach out and push her hair out of her face. I wanted to trace the outline of her full lips and kiss her one last time, but logically, I knew a clean break would be better for both of us. Or maybe it was just easier for me and I was taking the coward's way out. I'd purposely never gotten attached before for this very reason. Walking away was so much harder than I could ever imagine.

When Langley woke up alone, she was going to be pissed. As she had every right to be. I wouldn't blame her if she felt like I'd taken advantage of her. I never intended to, but then again, I never intended to like her—*really* like her—either. I figured pissed off was better than brokenhearted. I'd rather have her hate me for dipping out and leaving her high and dry, than have her pining and silently suffering while she waited for my return. If I returned. I couldn't do much for her now that our week was up and my time to serve had come, but I could leave her with something hot like anger, instead of something frigid and cold like loneliness and longing.

On silent feet, I prowled around the extravagant hotel room, steadily looking for the rest of the money Langley owed me. In my life, I'd done some things I wasn't exactly proud of, but searching for the cash while she slept soundly after a night of intimately learning every dip and curve of her body, was probably the lowest I'd ever felt. If Gael wasn't counting on the five grand for school, I would've slipped out the door and been on my way, but letting Langley down was bad enough. I couldn't disappoint my little brother as well. I wouldn't.

I found the money in her open suitcase, cringing as I tucked it away in my wallet. Rubbing my hands over my short hair, I looked back at the still form on the bed. A pang hit the center of my chest and I sucked in a breath against the sudden pain. Could I really disappear on her without saying a word? She'd already been screwed over so badly by the last guy she trusted. There was no way in hell I wanted her to lump me in the same category as that dick, Dick.

I blinked and jerked my hand back when I realized I was reaching for her involuntarily. My fingers were shaking so hard I had to curl my hands into fists to get the tremor under control. Swearing softly under my breath, I froze, a million words I needed to say stuck in my throat. Silently, I lowered my head and counted backward until I had myself under control.

As if she subconsciously felt the dark shift in the air, Langley rolled over, kicking her legs free of the comforter. The tiny frown between her golden brows was still there and her mouth pulled into an adorable mew of dissatisfaction. If she was dreaming, it wasn't about anything good. When she woke up, her reality was going to be something even worse.

Swearing softly again, I moved off the bed toward the built-in desk in the room. I found the small pad of Broadmoor stationery and the logoed pen. I was pretty good with words. Growing up in a rough, ugly neighborhood meant I learned to talk fast and use my words as weapons at a very early age. However, I was not a guy who had ever sat down and tried to pour his heart out onto a piece of paper. I couldn't remember a single time in my twenty-four years where I'd ever written a letter to another human being, let alone one who mattered to me. Even my text messages and emails tended to be short and to the point. I needed to do this for Langley. She deserved more than waking up alone to an empty bed. She needed to hear the whole story and understand *why* I couldn't offer her more, even though I was tempted to.

Using the faint glow of my cell phone screen, I jotted down several pages, pouring out my soul onto the paper in front of me. The words were one hundred percent honest, the unvarnished truth about why I was leaving, how I felt about going, and most importantly, why I'd kept the truth from her during the last week. I hoped she understood. I was fully prepared for her to hate me forever, letter or no letter. I jerked in the leather wingback chair I was sitting in when a single drop of moisture suddenly landed on the last page of my confession, smearing the ink and making my signature blur.

I scrubbed the heel of my palm over my cheek, stunned to find it wet. I wasn't exactly emotionally repressed or anything like that. I liked to think I was a modern enough guy, in touch with my feelings and aware of their impact. But, my life had never been a walk in the park. I was surrounded by extreme violence, and sadly, the loss of life on a regular basis...and that had been true for me even before I enlisted. It took a lot to move me to actual tears, but here I was, face damp, eyes blurry, because of a girl I'd only known for a week. Shaking my head at myself and at the situation, I pushed away from the desk, casting one last look in Langley's direction.

I would never admit it, but deep down, I knew I was hoping she would wake up before I ran away. I wanted to see those bright blue eyes one last time. I wanted her to chew me out and vent all the rage at me I was sure she was going to feel. I really wanted to kiss her, to fall back in bed with her, to keep her as my own. Too bad none of that was in the cards.

I left the letter and the tux behind. I wasn't going to need the monkey suit anytime soon. It was bad enough taking the money made me feel a little bit like a gigolo. I nearly tripped sneaking out the door because I swore I heard Langley call my name. I waited a split-second in silence, then practically ran down the hallway to the elevator. I felt like the world's biggest coward, but I'd convinced myself this was the right thing to do and there was no going back, now that I was out the door. Slinking out of the expensive hotel at dawn was officially one of the lowest points in my life. It twisted my guts and made my head pound in frustration.

It felt like it took a thousand years for the uniformed valet to bring my truck around. I kept waiting for Langley to appear out of thin air, or her father to show up, ready to kick my ass. It was what I would want to do if I knew some lowlife invaded my daughter's prestigious world, shook up her entire family, got her hopes up, then left her to deal with the fallout all on her own. Luckily, the only member of the wedding party I ran across was an obviously still-drunk bridesmaid whose morning walk of shame kept her head down and eyes averted.

I pounded on the steering wheel with the side of my fist as soon as I climbed in the truck. A heavy weight of wrongness settled on my shoulders, and I wanted to throw my head back and scream. I almost turned around and went back to the hotel twice. Luckily, my brother called when my willpower was at its lowest. I pulled into the parking lot of my apartment building and rested my head against the passenger window as Gael's voice came through the Bluetooth connected speakers.

"Are you okay, Ike?" His voice still sounded so young, so innocent. I would give my last breath to keep him that way. "I got a weird feeling and couldn't go back to sleep until I called you."

We'd always been weirdly connected in that way. My Spidey senses tingled when something was off with him as well. He was always extra anxious and on alert right before I deployed.

I cleared my throat. "You should be in bed, not worrying about me." I tried to keep my voice light, but failed miserably. "I'm really sorry I didn't make it home this time. But I'm glad you get to go to your dream school. I miss you and I'm not sure when I'll see you next. I guess I'm just bummed how things worked out."

Dealing with my first semi-broken heart was worth it as long as Gael was taken care of, and his future was secure.

There was only a day left before I officially deployed. I'd always planned to spend the last free week I had stateside with my family, but then the money thing had come up and I'd been left scrambling for a solution. The opportunity with Langley had been a lifesaver. I wanted to drive my truck down to Texas, so Gael could keep it and use it to move himself to school in the fall and hold onto until I got home, but now a friend was taking on the task for me, because my time was up.

"I miss you too. You sound funny. Are you sure you're all right?" His concern was practically palpable through the phone.

I grunted and rubbed my eyes. "Honestly, I've been better."

My brother made a soft sound. "Worried about the deployment?" If I wasn't mistaken, he was and wouldn't say it. He always worried about me when I was overseas, which was how I knew I didn't want to put anyone else important through that agonizing uncertainty.

"No. I'm worried about the people I'm leaving behind." I heaved a deep sigh and hit the steering wheel again. "I can't believe I'm not going to be there to see you move into the dorms. I missed so much of you growing up. You turned into an adult overnight on me."

My voice cracked a little and I felt the sting of moisture at the back of my eyes. Jesus. What had catching feelings for Langley Vaughn done to me? I was a sentimental mess.

Gael made a strangled sound which made my already tender heart twist painfully. "I don't want you to worry about me and Grandma. I want you to focus on yourself, so you come back safe and sound."

"Roger that. Go back to bed and let Grandma know I'll check in whenever I get the chance." I needed to get off the phone with him before I really broke down.

"Will do." I was about to disconnect the call when Gael called my name softly. "You still have to tell me how you suddenly came up with the money to pay for school. I know it has to do with why you didn't come home. That's a story I've been waiting to hear, ya know."

Smart kid. He always seemed to know there was more going on than what I was telling him.

"That story doesn't have a happy ending other than I got the money we needed, kiddo." My voice shook and there wasn't any way to hide it.

"If you're the one holding the pen, you're the one in charge of how the story ends. Don't forget that, Ike. Fly safe."

Damn. The kid always had to prove just how much brighter than me he was. I was going to be pondering his deep, insightful words the entire five-hour flight to the coast tomorrow. Grumbling about genius siblings and unfortunate dream girls, I made my way inside so I could finish packing my personal belongings I was going to take with me.

I was leaving without managing to say goodbye face-to-face to anyone who mattered the most to me. All I could do was I hope I made it home and got an opportunity to fix the litany of mistakes and misunderstandings I was leaving behind.

When there was more time, maybe I could make Langley...understand. She pretended her heart was bulletproof, but I had seen proof over the last week just how soft and vulnerable it really was.

Hopefully, by then, enough time would've passed that I would be able to figure out my complicated, convoluted feelings as well.

Because right now, I was clueless, and for the first time in a long time, feeling something that was lurking really close to the edge of regret.

Chapter 13

Langley

The world came into focus one blink at a time as the sleep cleared from my eyes. Through the bedroom window, I could tell the sun had risen, and thanked past me for choosing the suite that didn't face east.

Rolling slowly toward Iker, I stretched with closed eyes, my muscles protesting the movement.

My hand swept across the king-sized bed and only found a wide expanse of cool linen where I'd expected to find a couple hundred pounds of warm Iker.

My eyes confirmed what my touch assumed—he must already be awake. Not that I expected anything different. Dad told me he'd woken up at five a.m. for years after he'd gotten out of the military.

I sat up slowly, holding the sheet over my breasts and wincing from the tender areas awakening on my body before a smile slowly spread on my face. Last night had been incredible. The stuff of fairytales and epic romances.

"Hey, Iker, are you hungry? We could order room service," I called out, watching the bedroom door with giddy expectation. "Or we could forget breakfast all together."

I was more than down with that thought. I could even call the front desk and extend our stay so we could spend all day in bed together, which sounded utterly delicious. Then again, I wasn't sure a full day would even start to quell my obsession with him. I could probably spend the rest of my life in bed with him and possibly only scratch that surface.

And now we had that time, that possibility of the future.

"Iker?" Huh. The bedroom door was pretty thick, so if he was on the other side of the door, he probably couldn't hear me.

I swung my legs out of bed, cursing the heels I'd worn yesterday as my tired feet hit the floor, abandoned the bed sheet, and opened the door just enough to peek my head out. "Iker?"

There was no movement in the rest of the suite, and no answer. Chills swept over my naked body and I closed the door.

"He wouldn't..." I said aloud and then laughed. Of course he hadn't left. His tux was still draped over the chair. He had to have gone for a walk or coffee, or something to fill the time until I woke up. It was incredibly sweet of him to let me sleep.

I dressed quickly, pulling on a pair of shorts and a flowy tank from my suitcase. Thank God Camille hadn't insisted on one of those morning-after breakfasts. Not that I wouldn't get a kick out of seeing everyone hungover, but I'd had quite enough of...well, everyone.

Enough of doing what was expected of me instead of what was best for me.

Enough of the snarky comments from Virginia and Camille's need to one-up me at every turn.

Enough of feeling like I'd been squished into a box that couldn't contain me.

Enough of taking everyone's feelings into consideration before I even had a chance to explore my own.

And it was definitely time to explore. My mind raced as I brushed my hair and pulled it into a quick, messy bun. I could get an apartment near campus this week before the rest of the student body even thought about coming back. That would get me out of Dad's house, Virginia's line of fire, and the comfort of the sorority.

I would be independent for the first time in my life... except for the whole using-my-trust fund-to-pay-for-it thing, but that was money from my mom and she'd want me to be happy.

But I could also do something about that too. Not just finding out where Iker's little brother went to school and anonymously donating his tuition straight to his account, but other kids who hadn't grown up with my same advantages.

Hell, the interest on the account alone made enough to help someone else out who needed it.

I walked back into the bedroom feeling lighter than I had in years. And it was all because of Iker. His perspective and his strength, and his—

"Ow!" I yelped as something sharp bit the bottom of my foot. Leaning down, I found one of Iker's cufflinks that had scattered last night. I laughed, rubbing the sore spot on my foot, then gathered up the cufflink and its errant partner before walking out into the sitting room.

The platinum warmed in my hand and I grinned as I ran my thumb over the onyx inlay. They reminded me of Iker, which was why I'd bought them. The cool, hard exterior protected the warm, unfathomable center, which at the time had reminded me of his eyes, but now, his heart.

I came up short as I reached the dining room table. Our two keys lay side by side on the dark walnut. Hmmm. Good thing I'd woken up, or he would have been locked out.

But he wasn't absentminded enough to leave without a key. He was a contingency kind of guy.

Which meant he'd knowingly left without it.

My pulse leapt. *He wouldn't.*

I raced for my clutch and grabbed my phone. No text messages. No missed calls.

But he wouldn't have left without...

The cufflinks and my phone clattered when I dropped them on the table, but the noise barely registered over the roaring in my ears as I stumbled into the bedroom.

My suitcase—I hadn't noticed earlier, but I hadn't been looking either. Where was it? I looked once. Twice.

My stomach hit the floor, and then so did every piece of clothing I'd brought.

It wasn't here.

The envelope with the rest of money I owed Iker was gone.

Because *Iker* was gone.

I backed away from the suitcase slowly, and when the back of my knees hit the bed, I sat. My breaths were even and measured because I forced them to be. When my heart tried to stop beating, I sucked in air and forced my lungs to expand.

He'd left. Last night, he'd…

I shook my head, refusing to even *think* about last night. Then I dropped to my knees and picked up everything I'd thrown in my search. I was packed in five minutes, until I stood face-to-face with his tux.

He'd taken my money.

My body.

My *heart*.

All of which, I'd given him freely.

But he'd left behind the tux like it was a rental, when really, it was me who was obviously the rental.

I'd paid him for the week, and yet somehow, I felt like the whore.

He hadn't even said goodbye.

I left the tux just like he'd left me, draped prettily on the furniture, clueless that its use had been outlived. Damn, I was a great judge of character, not that I hadn't gotten exactly what I'd asked him for that first night. Hell, I'd even gotten a few orgasms as a bonus.

My clutch went into the front pocket of the suitcase. My phone slid into the back pocket of my shorts. And the cufflinks? Those could stay right where they were, just like every memory of Iker. I'd walk out of this hotel suite and leave him behind me. My friends had flings all the time, and they got away unscathed. I could too.

Then I saw it, the little pile of hotel-sized notepaper, sitting there at the head of the table. My legs carried me the distance, my hands reached for the stack, and my brain tried desperately to keep up.

When I saw his handwriting scrawled across the paper, I sank into the chair.

> Langley,
> I've been sitting here for ten minutes, trying to figure out what to say. When it comes down to it, there's nothing I can give you but the truth.
> Right now, you're asleep in that bed, naked, and warm, and so damned soft. All I want is to climb back in next to you and stay. Langley, despite all the odds, all I want is to stay. I hope you believe that. This week—last night. I'll never forget it. I'll never forget you.
> You're nothing I expected, nothing I wanted, and everything I needed. You walked into that bar in a dress that would stop traffic, and instead, you spun my world off its axis.
> I knew what I wanted before you walked in. I wanted to get Gael through school. I wanted to steer clear of any emotional attachments. I wanted to have a clear mind to lead and care for the soldiers in my squad. I wanted to be dependable and rock steady.
> You took care of number one—Gael. It's not your fault, but you kind of fucked the rest of that list for me.
> I got attached—to you.

My mind isn't clear—it's cluttered with thoughts of you.

I'm about to walk out this door, which means dependable is gone.

My hands aren't steady—they keep reaching for you. And now I'm worried they'll keep reaching from half a world away.

I'm leaving today. I'm about to be deployed.

I didn't tell you at first because I figured you never needed to know. We both had a clearly defined expiration date. You needed someone to get you through the wedding, it was never supposed to be more than that. But then it was.

It was you and your eyes. Your kiss in the hallway at your dad's. Your bare feet on the swing. Your stupid cold soup. Your laugh. Your class in the face of utter bullshit. It was walking through your world and realizing that while I grew up watching for people with real knives, you grew up watching for people carrying proverbial ones to stick in your back. I think I got the better end of that bargain—at least I can see them coming.

Something about us was different. This entire week was unlike anything I've ever experienced before.

I needed to tell you I was leaving, but I couldn't. Because, I saw past the labels and the money and you...you're worth more than all of it.

And I knew if I told you that I'm leaving for Afghanistan, you'd do exactly what you shouldn't. You'd wait for me.

Admit it, that's what you're thinking right now. Because that's who you are. You're loyal. You're kind. You hold onto things—to people—who are long gone. I cannot be someone you hold onto, because I can't do the same. Not because I don't want to, but because the distraction of missing you will compromise the lives I'm in charge of. And let's be honest, you don't belong in my world any more than I belong in yours. Yours would suffocate me, and mine would ruin you.

Call this what it is. What it was. An eclipse. A comet. Whatever. Something raw and rare that only comes around once in a lifetime that changes you—and then leaves.

You deserve freedom. Space. Time. Everything you could need to figure out who you are when you're not trying to be everyone you've been told you're supposed to be. You can't do that holding onto me. I won't be your garden swing.

I'm not going to lie. I hate your world. I hate that the gold here is really just plate, and when you scratch the surface, all the ugly is revealed. At least where I come from, people are real. I hate insults disguised as compliments. I loathe people who can't stay faithful and view sex as a tool for power or revenge. I'm disgusted by the casual cruelty that's so commonplace you've learned at such a young age that a $5,000 tuxedo should provide sufficient armor from your enemies. And yes, I looked up the cost of the armor you gave me.

But you... You're none of that. You're twenty-four karat to your soul, and no scratch will change that. You somehow survived swimming with the piranhas without becoming a shark. You gave me your body, your trust, and your honesty, and here I am, walking out while you're sleeping.

It's okay to hate me. It would be easier if you did. God knows I already hate myself.

I'm going to do everything I can to put you out of my mind and I hope you do the same. I'm nothing if not a survivalist.

But when I sleep, in those moments when I lose control of my thoughts, I know I'll be here again, sitting at this table. In my nightmares, I'll walk out the door, just like I'm about to do.

In my dreams, I'll still be in that bed with you.

~ Iker

My thumb caressed his blurred signature.

That noble, self-sacrificing, heart-stealing *asshole*.

He was deploying to a war zone. The man was literally going to war and hadn't told me, protecting me once again. Hadn't let me kiss him goodbye. Hadn't wanted me as a distraction—not that I blamed him.

My tears came quick and hard, until my chest shook with heaving sobs. I thought I'd known heartbreak. Turns out, I hadn't. I'd known disappointment and disillusionment, but not heartbreak. This gaping hole in my chest, the pain that forced its way out of my throat in a mournful cry, the simultaneous need to both run after Iker and tell him to fuck off...this was heartbreak.

Because somewhere in the last seven days, I'd fallen in love with him. And it wasn't the polite kind. Wasn't the society-approved kind. The cotillion-educated, well-bred, power-couple kind.

This was messy, and painful, and so much better because it was *real*. He was right. My world would either smother him or transform him—neither of which I could abide. His? He'd never shared enough of it with me to even answer how I could or couldn't adapt. So, he'd taken that decision away from me because he knew in his heart what my reaction would be. I'd wait for him, no matter how long it took.

We were misfits. We were the puzzle that took hours to put together only to realize there was a missing piece. We were the chipped wine glass, the knock-off designer purse, the misplaced cufflinks, the misspelled word in the final exam essay. We were so close to being...perfect, but couldn't make it past the test.

I gathered Iker's letter and the room keys in one hand, and tugged my suitcase behind me as I left the suite, closing the door with a soft *click*.

He was right. We were like a comet, bright and rare—and just out of reach of those who wanted to touch it.

And now we were done. I'd never see those beautiful, deep, dark eyes again, either because of his choice, or fate's. Nothing was certain in war. Panic swelled in my throat, and I muffled another sob with my fist.

I blinked, spun, and used the key to open the door. Within steps, I had the cufflinks in my hand. These, I would take. I would keep them to prove I'd held him, even if just for a few days.

But the rest...I would leave.

This time, as I exited the suite, I left the keys on the table just as he had, so I wouldn't be tempted to come back again. He'd decided to sever our connection, and left me without the respect of getting to choose or even having a say. Guess, in the end, he was just another guy preaching in a one-sided conversation, who expected me to listen and learn.

Ahh, there it was—the disappointment. The disillusionment.

I gave myself over to the loss, the emotions, the complete devastation, so I could remember this feeling, because I'd never put myself in the position to let it happen again. Then I closed the door and locked my heart, all in the same turn of a handle.

Chapter 14

Iker

I squinted against the glare of the sun and watched dispassionately as a line of soldiers in front of me loaded solemnly onto the bus waiting to take them to Peterson Air Force base. The atmosphere was heavy and serious, or at least it felt that way to me.

This was far from my first rodeo, but some of these guys were still kids, barely out of high school and had no idea just how drastically their lives were about to change. How their perception of war and the world we lived in was going to be forever altered. A few of these guys were the same age as Gael, and it reaffirmed my decision to do whatever I had to do to make sure I was the only Alvarez in our family putting his neck on the line.

I never wanted Gael to see the things I'd witnessed or know what it was like to have to fold a flag for someone's wife, someone's father. I didn't want him to have to bury his friends, or kill his enemies, or to be in a situation where he knew he was going to end up leaving behind the people he loved. If Gael was lucky enough to find a girl who shook him to his entire core and turned his world upside down in the span of a few seconds, I wanted him to be able to hold onto her, to get the chance to love her the way she deserved.

"Hey, Alvarez." My spine snapped straight when a hand landed on my shoulder and gave me a little shake. I looked over at another Staff Sergeant in my platoon, Nolan McGowen. We'd pinned rank the same day, and he was one of the few soldiers at Carson I'd gotten close to while I was stationed here. "I've been calling your name for five minutes. Where's your head at?"

It was in a ritzy hotel room with a pretty blonde I probably wasn't ever going to see again. I'd been so busy since the sun came up, I thought I was doing a decent job hiding how distracted I was today. Apparently not.

"Just running through my checklist. This last week was a little crazy and I feel like I'm forgetting something." I knew exactly what that *something*, or rather *someone*, was, but I wasn't about to pour my heart out when I knew McGowan was a newlywed who was facing being separated from his new wife for the first time. And it wasn't that I was forgetting—I was distracted because I couldn't forget. I knew none of us had it easy, and my story wasn't one that was unique. I was far from the first soldier to walk away to avoid heartbreak, mine *and* hers, down the line. I had an entire country's safety and security that came before my fleeting happiness.

"Time to get your game face on. Gotta lead these kids through the gates of hell and bring them all back." My shoulder was squeezed again as I nodded in agreement.

I was getting ready to ask if his guys and their bus was ready to go when my phone beeped with an incoming text message. Today was the last day the thing would be active until I returned stateside in nine months. Figuring it was my brother, I pulled it out of my pocket and nearly dropped the device on the ground when I saw Langley's name on the screen. She was the last person I thought I was going to hear from after the way I'd bailed on her, but as always, the girl was full of surprises.

Her message was short and sweet.

Langley: I'm really mad at you, but I still want you to stay safe. Take care of yourself, Iker.

A moment later, another text flashed across the screen, stealing my breath and making my heart hurt.

Langley: I'm not sure you'll see these messages, but I want you to know that until yesterday morning, this was the best week of my life. Thank you.

My thumbs itched to respond, to tell her the week had fundamentally changed me, that it had opened my eyes to what love could be really be like if you were willing to fight for it, to work at it. I wanted one last chance to remind her how incredibly special she was.

Instead, I powered the phone off and put it back in my pocket.

Now was not the time for me to think about being a boy in love as I was about to cross the threshold into a war zone.

No, right now, I had soldiers counting on me to make sharp, clear decisions. They were counting on me to keep them alive, and that responsibility had to come first. Love and war. Two powerful yet complicated beasts. How sad was it that I only had a grasp on how to deal with one and not the other? War was second nature. Love, however, was scary enough to send me running. I knew how badly war could hurt, but I was terrified of the way love might wound me.

Shoving down any lingering regret and remorse I had so deep inside of me I could feel it settle into my bones, I nodded at McGowan and walked toward the bus, leaving the fantasy and fairytale of the last week far behind. I was a soldier, first and foremost, not Prince Charming.

No matter how badly I wanted to play that role for Langley.

The End... for now!
Part II coming soon.

If you enjoyed *Girl in Luv*, be sure to preorder *Justified* by Jay Crownover. It releases in June and a preorder is the only way to get Part Two of Langley and Iker's love story.

The first three hundred readers who order a paperback copy of *Justified* and fill out the preorder form coming in April, are eligible for a signed/personalized copy of *Boy in Luv* (offer open internationally). *Boy in Luv* will be sent out to readers in late July.

All preorders, e-book, Audible, paperback... are eligible for a digital, e-book download as long as the form is filled out and proof of purchase is provided. This is a great deal! Technically, participants get three books for the price of one. You get *Justified*, the novella at the end of *Justified*, and a copy of *Boy in Luv*!

Amazon: http://bit.ly/JustifiedAMZ
B&N: http://bit.ly/justifiedBN
Apple: http://bit.ly/JustifiedApple
Kobo: http://bit.ly/JustifiedKobo
Goodreads: http://bit.ly/justifiedGR

Acknowledgements

First and foremost, I want to thank Rebecca. Thanks for agreeing to write a book with me. For helping me push it at readers. For dealing with my bossy, nitpicky personality. (I'm that way always, but when I work…oof…I wouldn't want to deal with me AT ALL… lol) Thanks for answering a million questions about military life in the middle of the night so Iker could be as authentic a hero as possible. Thanks for being the best neighbor and friend a gal could ask for. You're awesome…I mean it. One day, you'll believe me when I tell you that.

I love my editor, Elaine York. I love how she makes each book I send her better, and forces me to think harder, longer, deeper about each story we work on together. She's the best. She also makes the guts of my books really pretty, so she's basically my secret weapon!

Thank you to Jenn Wood for digging in and copyediting GIL! Sorry I'm the world's worst at writing run-on sentences. I'd say it's part of my charm, but really, I know it is just annoying…lol.

Also, thank you to Mayhem Cover Creations for making the outside of the book as beautiful as the inside.

Shout out to my team, Mel, Stacey, and KP. Girls rule the world and none of these words would be in your hands without these wonderful women I get to work with day in and day out.

Lastly, the biggest thanks goes out to the readers who pre-ordered *The Last Letter* and *Justified* so they could experience this co-writing journey with Rebecca and me in real time. Thank you for trusting us to give you a great story. Thank you for your support. Thank you for your excitement...thank you for reading! YOU ARE AMAZING... Just wait until book two!!!!

Acknowledgments, take two:

First up, thank you to Jason for being the soldier I met in a bar nineteen years ago. You still get me, baby.

Next, and bigger thanks, goes to Jay, not just for the sheer amazingness of you writing this with me, but for suggesting it in the first place. For putting your name next to mine. For giving me a safe, quiet space whenever I needed it. For answering every time I call even though you hate the phone. For driving the minivan when necessary and never forgetting a kid at cross-country practice while pulling off your best nanny impression. For showing up time and again and making me do the same. For being the wolf to my rabbit, and the tough love when I've had it with the universe. Secret's out, lady. You're a pineapple. Also, I'm not saying that I haven't forgiven you for the K-pop docu-drama experience of 2018, but I am saying you may have forfeited all movie choices for the next five years.

Thank you to my kids, who managed to break only one bone between the six of you while I wrote this with Jay. I really appreciate the decreased time at the orthopedist, so let's keep that up, shall we? In all honesty, you are the best of me and teach me far more than I could ever hope to teach you.

Elaine, thank you for editing this for us and making sense out of our little co-written baby! Jenn, thank you for copyediting and not mocking me for my love affair with commas. LJ, I adore our cover, and every other one you've done for me! KP, I can't decide if you're the luckiest publicist ever because you have both of us...or if I should send you cases of wine to deal with our shenanary. You are amazing, not just for what you do, but for the class with which you do it. Shelby, thank you for chasing my squirrels. I'd promise you to keep them under control, but we both know that would be a lie. Here's to the military guys we love.

To the readers, man, you guys ROCK for coming on this little trip with us. Thank you for preordering *The Last Letter* just so you could be here. Now go snag *Justified,* because you know you have to see how this one plays out. Also, let's be clear: Jay made me spell it that way. She also dresses my daughter in K-pop shirts, yeah...it's easier if you just smile and nod. ;)

About the Authors

MEET JAY CROWNOVER

NEW YORK TIMES & USA TODAY BESTSELLING AUTHOR Jay Crownover is the international and multiple *New York Times* and *USA Today* bestselling author of the Marked Men series, The Saints of Denver series, The Point series, Breaking Point series, and the Getaway series. Her books can be found translated in many different languages all around the world. She is a tattooed, crazy-haired Colorado native who lives at the base of the Rockies with her awesome dogs. This is where she can frequently be found enjoying a cold beer and Taco Tuesdays. Jay is a self-declared music snob and outspoken book lover who is always looking for her next adventure, between the pages and on the road.

This is the link to join my amazing fan group on Facebook: https://www.facebook.com/groups/crownoverscrowd … I'm very active in the group, and it's often the best place to find all the latest happenings including: release dates, cover reveals, early teasers, and giveaways!

My website is:_www.jaycrownover.com… there is a link on the site to reach me through email. I would also suggest signing up for my newsletter while you're there! It's monthly, contains a free book that is in progress so you'll be the first to read it, and is full of mega giveaways and goodies. I'm also in these places:

https://www.facebook.com/jay.crownover
https://www.facebook.com/AuthorJayCrownover
Follow me @jaycrownover on Twitter
Follow me @jay.crownover on Instagram
Follow me on Snapchat @jay crownover
https://www.goodreads.com/Crownover
http://www.donaghyliterary.com/jay-crownover.html

MEET REBECCA YARROS

Rebecca Yarros is a hopeless romantic and a lover of all things coffee and chocolate. She is the author of the award-winning Flight & Glory series and The Renegades. She loves military heroes, and has been blissfully married to her Apache pilot for seventeen years.

When she's not writing, she's tying hockey skates for her four sons, sneaking in guitar time, or watching brat-pack movies with her two daughters. She lives in Colorado with her husband, their rambunctious gaggle of kids, and their menagerie of pets. Having adopted their youngest daughter from the foster system, Rebecca is a passionate advocate for children through her non-profit, One October.

Join my reader group for exclusives, giveaways, the latest info, teasers, and shenanigans!: https://www.facebook.com/groups/RebeccaYarrosFlygirls/
Follow me on Facebook: www.facebook.com/rebeccaelizabethyarros

Follow me on Twitter: https://twitter.com/RebeccaYarros
Follow me on Instagram: https://www.instagram.com/rebeccayarros/
For deleted scenes, blogs about our insane little life, and my signing schedule, hop over to Rebeccayarros.com!

Made in the USA
Monee, IL
27 July 2025